The Last Client
of Luis Montez

ALSO BY MANUEL RAMOS

The Ballad of Rocky Ruiz
The Ballad of Gato Guerrero

MANUEL RAMOS

The Last Client
of Luis Montez

◆

ST. MARTIN'S PRESS
NEW YORK

Library of Congress Cataloging-in-Publication Data

Ramos, Manuel.
    The last client of Luis Montez / by Manuel Ramos.—1st ed.
        p.   cm.
    ISBN 0-312-13997-7
    1. Mexican Americans—Colorado—Denver—Fiction. 2. Lawyers—Colorado—Denver—Fiction. 3. Denver (Colo.)—Fiction. I. Title.
    PS3568.A4468L3   1996
    813'.54—dc20   95-39102
                                                                CIP

First Edition: March 1996

10   9   8   7   6   5   4   3   2   1

Traigo una pena clavada,
como puñalada en mi pensamiento.
Como carcajada que se hace lamento
como si llorando se rieran de mí.
Es la vida pasada que siento
reprochar el haber sido así.

—"Mi Unico Camino" (D.A.R.)

For the grandparents: Antonia Ramos De Larosa, Manuel Ramos, Tom De Larosa; Filomena Sarmiento, Manuel Sarmiento with respect and cariño.

Very special thanks to ace legal advisers Warwick Downing and Guillermo Garibay; for timely assistance, Mercedes Hernández and Rudy Garcia; to the man in San Diego, MCPO José (Pepe) Hernández; and, of course, Flo.

Prologue

DISTRICT COURT, CITY AND COUNTY OF DENVER,
COLORADO
Criminal Action No. ATA-789, Courtroom 9

ORDER

THE PEOPLE OF THE STATE OF COLORADO,
Plaintiffs,
v.
JAMES P. ESCH,
Defendant

This matter comes before the Court on defendant's motion to suppress evidence. The Court, having heard testimony and weighed the evidence, and being fully apprised, makes the following findings of fact and conclusions of law:

On the night of April 11, 1992, Officers Ben Martinez and Thomas Strayhorn were on regular patrol in the northwest quadrant of the city and county of Denver. Around midnight, they observed a vehicle "weaving between traffic lanes and running a red traffic signal." The officers attempted to make a traffic stop of the vehicle, but the automobile did not pull over until it arrived at a deserted shopping center parking lot.

Strayhorn testified that as the officers approached the automobile from their own car, he saw one of the passengers in the rear seat of the car "stuff something under the front seat." Until that point, the sole reason for the stop was the erratic performance of the car's driver. Strayhorn requested a backup unit when he saw the activity of the passengers.

The driver identified himself as Alton Enoch. The defendant, James P. Esch, the passenger in the backseat, could not produce identification when one was requested by Officer Strayhorn. The other passenger in the car, Enoch's girlfriend, Glory Jane Jacquez, provided the officers with identification.

Although there was a conflict in the evidence, there is no doubt that Officer Strayhorn ordered all three out of the car. He searched under the front seat and, on the passenger's side, found a leather bag, secured with a leather thong and decorated with beads and rhinestones. Officer Strayhorn then testified, and I quote from the transcript of his testimony, that he "manipulated the bag" and, although he "did not feel any weighty objects or things like a gun," he untied the leather thong and opened the bag "to check for weapons and possible identification." Strayhorn and Martinez also testified that when the bag was opened, defendant Esch said, "The bag's mine." In the bag, Strayhorn found Esch's driver's license and two small envelopes with a powdery substance. Strayhorn advised Esch that he would have the substance tested, at which point Esch said, "Fuck that, man. You know it's coke." The other occupants of the automobile shouted at Esch to stop talking, and all three were placed under arrest. (The Court notes that although the other two have been charged with offenses stemming from the arrests on the night of April 11, 1992, those cases have not been consolidated with this action.) No weapons were found in the car, and the defendants refused to make any additional statements to the police. Defendant Esch eventually was charged with possession of a controlled substance (cocaine).

It is clear to the Court that the officers had no probable cause or reasonable grounds to suspect that the leather bag contained cocaine, or any other drug. There is not one piece of evidence to justify any such conclusion. However, the officers would have been justified in searching the bag if they had a reasonable belief based on specific and articulable facts that the suspects were dangerous and had access to weapons. In *Michigan* v. *Long,* 463 U.S. 1032 (1983), the Supreme Court held that police officers may conduct a "protective search" for weapons, not only of the driver but also of the vehicle.

The *Long* case has been applied to cases in Colorado, and certain standards have been established by the Colorado appellate courts, primarily in the opinions that have become known as *Cagle I* and *Cagle II*. See *People* v. *Cagle*, 688 P.2d 718 (Colo. 1984), and *People* v. *Cagle*, 751 P.2d 614 (Colo. 1988), appeal dismissed sub nom. *Cagle* v. *Colorado*, 486 U.S. 1028 (1988). Under these standards, this Court is satisfied that Officers Strayhorn and Martinez had an articulable and specific basis for stopping the automobile. The traffic offenses were constitutional justification for the intrusion by the police officers. The furtive conduct of the passengers as the officers approached was an obvious, potentially dangerous response that required a call for backup.

The critical issue is whether the search of the bag had a reasonable relationship to the stated purpose of the search— i.e., ensuring the officers' safety. It is on this issue that the search fails to meet constitutional standards. The testimony of Officer Strayhorn indicated that he had no reasonable concern for his safety. The defendants were cooperating; they were outside the car, under the watchful eye, and weapon, of Officer Martinez, and Strayhorn's "pat-down" search of the bag did not turn up any indication of a weapon. The search of the bag exceeded the constitutionally permissible bounds of the limited protective search of the passenger compartment of an automobile.

The Fourth Amendment to the Constitution prohibits unreasonable searches and seizures. The search of the leather bag and subsequent seizure of the envelopes were unreasonable under the Fourth Amendment. Therefore, evidence discovered on the basis of the unlawful search or seizure must be suppressed (the "poisonous tree"), as well as any derivative evidence ("fruit of the poisonous tree"). Defendant Esch's statements are the fruit. They would not have been made if the illegal search of the bag had not occurred.

This Court deeply regrets its findings, but there is no other choice, given the testimony of the officers, particularly Strayhorn, and the arguments made by defense counsel. This Court is well aware of Mr. Esch. His criminal record is before the Court, and in bulk and weight alone it is impressive. There are times when the law leaves little room for common sense or practical reality.

Therefore, this Court orders that the contents of the leather bag, as well as all of defendant Esch's statements after the search of the bag was begun, are hereby suppressed.

DONE AND SIGNED IN OPEN COURT THIS 14TH DAY OF JANUARY, 1993.

By the Court:

_____

District Court Judge

Part I

1

―――――――――――◆―――――――――――

Can we get together?"

Lisa's voice put something into that innocent phrase that would have made me blush had my skin been a shade or two lighter.

I took it as a sign. Maybe that playful imp—fate—had decided to line me up one more time. Falling back on nonsense was something I wouldn't hesitate to do if it fit the moment.

"I'll pick you up in an Explorer—lilac and black. You can't miss it. Four-wheel drive, so I don't get stuck in the drifts."

I tried to focus on the details so I wouldn't have to call her back and ask what it was she had said, but it was tough.

"I want to thank you, Louie, personally. For helping Jimmy. But I won't be free until this afternoon. Maybe we can have coffee, or a drink?"

I agreed to meet Lisa after my 2:00 P.M. hearing with Judge Frederick.

My court appearance was a waste of time. The heating system wasn't all it should have been for the justice center

3

of a major American city. So many clerks, bailiffs, and secretaries had stayed home that the judges who had driven into town were quick to cancel what they could and dispose of everything else as unceremoniously as possible. Judge Frederick agreed with the red-nosed, sniffling deputy district attorney that because one of the witnesses against my client had slid into three other cars along Sixth Avenue, on her way into court, the preliminary hearing should be rescheduled.

I protested, mumbling something about my client's right to a speedy trial, but after Frederick rolled his eyes, I flourished my pocket calendar and graciously agreed on a date for the next hearing.

I spent more than an hour roaming the almost-deserted halls of the courthouse, gabbing with an occasional clerk, until I broke down and bought a cup of coffee in the basement cafeteria. Then I exchanged raunchy jokes with a sleepy guard stationed at the Bannock Street entrance's metal detector. Slightly warmed, I ventured into the muck to wait for my ride.

I had proposed that I wait for Lisa at the corner of Bannock and Colfax Avenue, outside the courthouse, so that she wouldn't have to hassle parking. My frozen butt didn't let me forget the foolishness of my chivalrous gesture.

For a reason that became more obscure the longer I shivered on the corner, I was in a public-transportation state of mind, and I had neglected my car for most of the winter. I had intended to borrow Priscilla's car, since my secretary's medium-sized Chevy was far more reliable in the snow than any auto I could get my hands on. But that would have inconvenienced her, particularly as she wanted to get home as soon as she could. I couldn't think of a good reason to keep her twiddling her thumbs in my office, and when Lisa's husky voice offered to be my chauffeur, I struck a deal with my bored secretary. If she gave me a ride downtown to the

4

hearing, she could take off the rest of the day. The blizzard had slowed business, and there were only so many files that Priscilla could file away, and only so many times she could rearrange the chairs in my waiting room.

It was also the least I could do for the environment. Red pollution days were supposed to mean that people joined in car pools, didn't burn wood, and, generally, cut back on anything that might add more particulates to the atmosphere. I was as civic-minded as the next guy—even more so when my thoughtfulness involved a petite redhead with what I knew to be a fairly liberated outlook on life and what I imagined to be a well-entrenched need to express her appreciation.

At 3:30 in the afternoon, cold long shadows draped across the skyline, covered the parking lots, and darkened most of downtown Denver. The streets were cold; the buildings were cold; I was cold. The January air whipped through the canyons of the skyscrapers, then aimed straight for me. Gusts twirled around my legs, raising bits and pieces of ice that clung to my heaviest pair of wool slacks. I inhaled coldness through clenched teeth. Frigid slivers of oxygen and pollutants knifed down my throat and into my lungs. A drop of moisture stubbornly clung to the numb tip of my nose, and I ached like an old miner. I coughed and wheezed.

Although I stood in semidarkness, the sky overhead was bright with sunshine that accented the crisp arctic blue. I tried to tell myself that maybe the winter wasn't so tough. That lasted as long as it took for the minus-fifteen-degree windchill factor to overcome my overcoat and layers of shirts and sweaters, and for my toes to cringe and cramp with each step in the crusted snow.

The storm had spent itself on the Mile High City two days before. Its memory was alive and well on dangerous sidewalks and in uncooperative car batteries, and enhanced by the irritability of court clerks, waiters, bus drivers, and any-

5

one else I had to come into contact with during my daily sorties into the real world of the last major storm of Colorado's winter.

Ice encased my mustache. When Lisa's all-purpose vehicle finally rolled in front of me, I would have sworn that sections of my face were falling off in dark, frozen chunks. Her car sloshed through a three-foot hill of gray and black gunk that at one time had been snow cleared from the middle of Colfax Avenue. She expertly eased it to a pause without too much of a slide, then idled at the curb.

The window tint was almost black, and a thick coat of ice and mud smeared across the glass except where the wipers scraped a crazy pattern of lines and semicircles. Lisa was a blurry phantom behind the steering wheel. She might have waved at me, so I opened the door and stepped into a bucket seat.

Heat engulfed me as soon as I sat down. The heater's hum reassured me and I felt a tad more alive. And there was Lisa, too. Her smell—her taste—must have been part Amarige, part sweat, and maybe a shot or two of apricot schnapps. She smiled from beneath wraparound sunglasses and a Day-Glo teal ski jacket designed to turn heads on the steepest slopes in Steamboat. Her hair was bundled under a knit cap, but stray shiny strands flicked around her neck and across her forehead.

Only Lisa could cause a hot flash in freezing weather.

"Sorry I'm late. The streets are still a mess. Hope you didn't get too cold." Before I could answer, she added, "I know a place where you can warm up. We can talk."

"You're the driver."

She eased into the sluggish traffic and expertly changed lanes so she could turn around and end up back on Colfax, heading west. A country-western station broadcast the latest storm alerts, with needless warnings to listeners to "be careful out there, y'all," then went into "ten in a row." I tuned out the saccharine songs and focused on Lisa. She concentrated on keeping her vehicle on the street, without spinning on the ice or ending up stuck in mud and snow. I didn't want to distract her. Straining against her Colorado status symbol in order to free it from a drift was not on my agenda for that afternoon. Not for any afternoon.

Keeping focused on Lisa was not difficult. She swallowed attention like a black hole in outer space seizes the light. Her classic cover-girl smile generated a high energy level, a reflection of her animated personality. Her body had been in constant motion whenever I had talked with her, and she'd had a hell of a time staying quiet during Jimmy's court proceedings. Quick, with an ironic sense of humor, she had a hundred ideas, plans, and motives bouncing around the inside of her head at once, and sometimes they included a few minutes with me, her brother's lawyer.

The People of the State of Colorado v. *James P. Esch* had to rank as one of my major achievements as a lawyer. Not that there were many, but once in a while Luis Montez, Esq., truly figured out this legal stuff, and his clients sometimes actually won.

Lisa's bar of choice was a cluttered tavern near Union Station that had experienced a resurgence of popularity along with the rest of lower downtown Denver. The ride to the Skyline Café & Saloon should have been slow and easy. But men such as I know that women such as Lisa never do anything slow and easy. The normal, most direct route to the bar, the Twentieth Street Viaduct, had been erased in the interest of the new baseball stadium, so Lisa had to steer through an elaborate and complicated detour behind the massive post office building. Construction on the stadium had torn up acreage, strewn trucks, cranes, and heavy equipment in haphazard patterns that might have made sense to a construction foreman, and generally screwed up access to the Skyline. Snow, mud, and ice added to the misery. The Skyline had better be a great bar.

Lisa cut off more careful drivers, splashed pedestrians dodging for protection, and eventually we landed in a pile of snow that should have been a parking space for the Skyline's customers. A crazy thought crossed my mind that maybe having a drink or two wasn't quite appropriate, but then I rationalized that the holiday season wasn't that far gone, and anyway, Lisa wanted conversation. The crazy thought gasped and died without any real shot at a meaningful life as Lisa and I chugged through the snow. I can talk myself into just about anything, when I put my heart behind it.

She took off her cap and her long, bright hair tumbled around her shoulders. We hung our coats on wall hooks and dropped gloves and scarves into a booth while our chilled senses adjusted to the bar's ambience.

Cigarette smoke and Texas white-boy blues floated around us in a nice mix of midafternoon booziness and insolent lethargy left over from the previous night. An amazing array of beer posters plastered the rough-hewn wooden walls, while numerous odd gadgets and trinkets left by patrons over the half a dozen years of the Skyline's existence dangled from the walls or across the back of the bar. Black corrugated tin carelessly covered the ceiling. I caught myself watching for it to fall on our heads.

We ordered drinks, and then I launched into the small talk.

"The weather doesn't seem to have hurt business."

She smiled, and I considered warning her to cut it out. I didn't.

She said, "This place always has a good crowd. A blizzard doesn't mean diddly to these people."

Denverites could party anytime, anywhere. That was my excuse, anyway.

"I never got a chance to really thank you, Louie. Jimmy's

8

such a screwup. I know it wasn't easy, what you did. It took a lot of hard work. He probably didn't say it, but the family appreciates it. . . . I appreciate it."

"Your parents back on speaking terms with Jimmy? I thought they'd disowned him for good."

"They can't. That's how they are. The old man blusters and preaches, but in the end, Jimmy is still his 'little guy'— the kid they think will one day snap out of it and grow up, if he doesn't get himself shot or fucked up some other way first. Sorry. I don't want to sound too pitiful. It's not my style." The shrug of her slender shoulders made me admire her style, whatever it was. "I can imagine what you think of the Eschs."

She drained her glass of schnapps and then sipped some kind of dark English ale whose name I had missed. I nursed my domestic long-neck. I was wary. I had seen too much of the Esch family dynamics. Working on my defense for James P. Esch, I had learned plenty about the family. I harbored a nagging suspicion that I had learned entirely too much for the ultimate well-being of one almost-over-the-hill, overworked, and tired Chicano attorney. I would always associate the name Esch with spoiled kids, political and financial scandal, a fairly wretched personal tradition, and money. My kind of clients.

"Hey, I'm a lawyer. I make a living off the disasters of my fellow human beings. That's why we put up with lawyer jokes—tit for tat. If lawyers were actually offended by the jokes, we would have sued someone to shut up the so-called comedy."

She gave me a polite giggle but didn't say anything.

"Lisa, you may not want to believe this, but I like Jimmy. I mean, for a spaced-out coke addict with absolutely no conscience, and the ability to attract lowlifes and bring out the worst in people, he's got a certain charm. Know what I mean?"

This time, she didn't even giggle. The smile turned down a notch or two. A young couple wearing army-surplus parkas and what we used to call engineer boots stomped through the doorway, and icy air swirled around them. The air matched the change in Lisa's mood and found its way to our booth.

"His addictions aren't funny, Louie. He's been through every program there is, even tried a guru in Boulder who channeled Jim Morrison. But I still remember my little brother, before the drugs, and everything else he got into."

"I suppose he was an angel, destroyed by material possession, a classic education, and the good life in general."

I wasn't trying to be sympathetic.

She shrugged again, and her downer mood was gone.

"Jimmy has always been a jerk. It's just that once he was a sober jerk. That was long ago."

She reached across the table and held my hand. Her warmth knocked the breath out of the winter. I expected sunny days, soon. Colorado will do that—freezing one day, a glorious spring the next. Maybe it was Lisa's fault.

"You're a nice guy, Louie. I'm glad Dave Padgett referred Jimmy's case to you. It was the best thing that's happened to Jimmy lately. And to me, too."

The eyes across the table were pretty and soft. I tried to fight it off, but I thought I saw a promise of sweet desire. The lines and edges that surrounded her eyes hinted at another side of Lisa. She had had the same upbringing as her brother, and look what he'd accomplished. How had she avoided her brother's fate—or had she? Then I silently rebuked myself for getting carried away with the negative vibes.

She massaged my palms and rubbed my fingers. She was seducing me, and I thought I might go along with it.

As if nothing intimate was happening between us, I

chattered on about her brother's case, and my job as a lawyer.

"Strictly speaking, the case isn't over, Lisa. The judge granted my motion to suppress. The DA can't use the drugs the cops found in the car, or the statements Jimmy and his friends made the night they were arrested. The DA's going to file an interlocutory appeal on the evidence question. He has to. There is no case without the evidence that the court ruled was inadmissible. If the state supreme court reverses Judge Bernstein, we're back where we started. I've got to win the appeal to keep Jimmy out of prison."

Lisa's fingers traveled up the sleeve of my jacket and unbuttoned my shirt cuff. Her fingers did crazy things to my wrist. She had found an erogenous zone I didn't know existed.

"You'll win, Louie. I read the judge's decision. There was no doubt you had him where you wanted him. You'll do the same with this appeal. I have faith in you. I trust you."

The young woman who had brought our first round of drinks sauntered near our table, and I noticed for the first time her black lipstick and fingernail polish. She asked if we wanted more drinks. Before we answered, she was distracted by the intensity of our hand-holding. She sighed and walked away.

It's a horny world, man. It's a place I know well.

Lisa had a fetish for country-western music. All her radios were fixed on stations that filled her need for spoon-fed emotion and simple sincerity, with a hint of a rural drawl. So at eight in the morning, a loud and boorish disc jockey yodeled for us to "roll out of the sack, hit the streets, and be careful out there, y'all."

I was curled up against Lisa's ass, covered with flannel sheets and down quilts, both of us naked. I groaned, refusing to believe that I had to wake up. The morning-show host was cut off in midyodel when the radio was rudely silenced. I reached for Lisa, but she was out of the bed. She had flicked off the radio, thrown a robe across her back, and said something about coffee. I heard her run down the flight of stairs. Our night had been filled with the requisite sexual acrobatics, and I needed to rest. I could hear Lisa bouncing around her house with energy to spare.

A faint ray of morning peeked around the decorator blinds of a large fan-shaped window that framed a totally white Longs Peak. Lisa lived by herself in a northwest suburb, in a new home with vaulted ceilings, three gas fireplaces, and an acre of kitchen. Looking around the bedroom for the first time, I noticed details: a picture of Greg and Beatrice Esch—Mom and Dad; neatly arranged country-western CDs on a shelf near her miniature music system; a Baggie of marijuana on the nightstand. The box of condoms I had frantically reached for in the subdued glow of Lisa's night-light nestled at the foot of the bed.

I raised my arms over my head and stretched my muscles until they protested with a slight twinge. I slowly stepped out of the bed, hunted down my clothes, and tried to make something of myself in Lisa's bathroom. The results were not good. Harried, overweight, out of shape, and full of aches and pains, the guy in the mirror deadpanned, "You're an old man, Montez."

Old and pathetic.

My breakup with Evangelina had etched itself in the grooves of my lamentable body. I missed her as though I'd lost my sense of sight, as though my eyes had been ripped out by a grotesque mythical griffin sent to wreak havoc on men who foolishly allow their hearts to break over love. From boss to lover was a long, untidy jump, but one I made with nostrils flaring and mouth agape. Hopeless.

I'd fallen hard, but in my suave and cosmopolitan fashion, I'd easily screwed it up. I used every excuse I could imagine in order to keep happiness at bay—our relationship had ruined a good friendship; we knew too much about each other from working together every day; she was beginning to learn what her life could be, while I regretted learning anything new about life, already knowing too much as it was. It came down to the fact that I was so set in my ways that the months we lived together were probably the best and the worst, and I just couldn't handle it. She finally threw in the towel, packed up, and headed to Los Angeles.

Her good-bye included one final jab.

"Louie, it's not happening for me anymore. You'll be part of me, always, you know that, but that's not enough. If you're ever in L.A., don't try to find me."

And I'd thought we were friends.

The time with Lisa had been a welcome break from my usual companions—rented movies and six-packs. But I couldn't get away from Evangelina. My dark, brooding ex-secretary may have left the state, but somehow she hovered over me in Lisa's bedroom, shaking her head in pity as I went through the motions. I concentrated, I did, and the sex had accomplished its purpose. Love on the rebound had a certain substance, not entirely unpleasant. For a time, Evangelina had ceased to exist. But then I looked up from the squirming Lisa and saw Evie in the corner, wearing that smirk I had dreamed about during those interminable bourbon-and-beer nights that glorified my loneliness.

When would I get this woman thing right? The memory of Evangelina wouldn't leave. Every song on the radio related to something she used to do; every scene in a movie tied into something about us. I dwelled on remembering her jabs about my ineptness around the house. Insignificant tasks she did loomed magnificently on the horizon of my wrecked world: correcting letters, briefs, and motions for my cases; acting out the role of the formal and businesslike secretary in front of clients, then climbing all over me as soon as we were alone in my office—her eyes, hands, tongue doing things that made me breathe hard and quickly lock the door to secure our privacy.

I found one of her socks at the bottom of my closet. Her romance novels lay forlorn on bookshelves. I'd see her car a block ahead and race to catch her, only to find a worried grandmother suspiciously eyeing the speeding wild man who screeched to a halt next to her. A tape of our favorite Mexican love songs punished me every time I looked for music to play—I couldn't bring myself to listen to it. Most of the time, I resorted to old blues. Elmore James and Ma Rainey did their best to make me feel better by singing about their own problems.

There were nights, softened with alcohol, when it worked. I vowed to go out and find another woman, to excise Evangelina's spirit, to carry out that old expression about filling the hole in my life with another nail from my coffin, or something like that.

Lisa returned with a cup of coffee. She flicked her lips across my cheek and then disappeared into the adjoining bathroom. I gulped the coffee, found her bedroom phone, and dialed my home message number. The office could wait. The background sounds of Lisa's shower tweaked my libido, but, on second thought, I wasn't sure I could maneuver in a shower stall anymore.

"Mr. Montez, I, uh . . . I just got a call for you from . . . from Denver General." Priscilla insisted on calling me Mr. Montez. "I don't know where you are. I hope you'll get this. It's your father. They took him late last night with some kind of heart thing, or something—oh, I don't know, I'm sorry, I don't know how to do this. It sounds serious, Mr. Montez. You better get over there. They've been trying to reach you."

Almost at the same instant, Lisa broke out into an old Hank Williams tune, the water stopped, and the shower door clicked shut. I chugged the rest of the coffee.

I was about to hang up when Priscilla's barely audible voice returned and forced me to keep the phone at my ear. Lisa casually walked into the bedroom, and out of the corner of my eye I watched her hands vigorously run a towel through her wet hair and over her naked body, glossy with lotion.

"A man named Tenorio was here when I opened the office. He was very upset, and crude. He said he came by yesterday, too, but we were all gone. Said he needs to talk to you about the Esch case—today. Something about an Officer Strayhorn and an accident, or something. He's a detective, an investigator, something. Oh, I don't know. Please, Mr. Montez, what am I supposed to do? Where are you?"

2

I stumbled into the lobby of Denver General, wearing the rumpled suit from the previous day's aborted courtroom appearance and sporting my normal bloodshot eyes, with added highlights from my night with Lisa. A nurse tried to explain what had happened, but she only exacerbated my concern, and confusion. I half-expected the skinny Chicana who patiently avoided my unintelligible questions to call a guard and have me dragged up to 4-West for a seventy-two-hour hold and observation.

"Your father has a long record of lung problems. He worked around coal dust for years, right?"

"Is that what this is, his lungs?"

"And Dr. Webster has tried for years to get Mr. Montez to take it easy with the food he eats. There's a lot of pressure on his heart."

"Shit, his heart! Is that what this is? His heart, or his lungs?" My voice was rising with my panic. "What's wrong with my father? I don't need his entire medical history—I already know that!"

"Please, Mr. Montez. I'll have to ask you to calm down."

"Look, uh . . ." The first name on the plastic ID tag pinned to the front of her small chest was Clara, naturally. I didn't feel friendly enough to use it. "Look, Ms. Knudson, I just want to know what happened. Why is my father here?"

"The ambulance brought your father in yesterday afternoon. Apparently, he was shoveling snow from his sidewalk with some neighbor boys when he collapsed. Dr. Webster will fill you in. He's ordered tests. But there was fluid in your father's lungs, and he complained about chest pains. He's stabilized. You can see him, but only for a few minutes."

I waited for directions to his room.

She cleared her throat.

"Mr. Montez. Your father is *very* sick. He's frail and not in general good health. He could be here for a while."

She quit speaking, and I hated the silence more than her bureaucratic evasion. Her eyes strayed to mine and then dropped to study the cracks in her clipboard. It was a nurse's way of saying what only doctors are supposed to verbalize. Jesús was in deep trouble, and if he didn't stay in the hospital for a while, it would be most likely because he had died.

I put up with more preliminaries, including some paperwork, and finally got the go-ahead to visit my father.

The old man was sleeping in his dark room, hooked up to tubes and machines. I quietly inched my way to the side of his bed. A century ago, when I was a boy, someone had taught me not to make noise in a hospital, unless I wanted information from a patronizing nurse. But Jesús Genaro Montez had picked up on the swish of the door as it swung shut behind me. Now his eyes fluttered open. Flabby face muscles worked hard to focus on me.

I had preserved an image of my father—a short, robust man with thick shoulders and stubby, powerful hands. He had roughhoused and wrestled with his children, not reluctant to use the strength he needed in the mines and on the construction scaffolds where he earned the money for our food and clothes. Often, we were forced to surrender, and I remember running in tears to our mother because Dad had broken my puny hold on his leg and sent me flying across the room.

The old man was tough. He had rarely told any of his children about his life as a young man, but I had picked up enough over the years to suspect that whatever wildness I might occasionally exhibit was only a hint at what he once had pulled off.

Tucked beneath the crisp hospital sheets and among the beeping trappings of medical technology, he looked diminutive and weak. The fear grabbed me at that instant. I reached for his hands and tried to smile. I'm not the right guy for this, I thought.

"Dad."

I think he smiled in return, but it might have been an attempt to laugh. I had always amused my father. His voice was scratchy and dim.

"It's about time, Louie. Were you going to wait until they needed someone to identify the body?"

He was glad to see me.

"I came as soon as I found out. I left the office early yesterday and I was kind of out of touch, but Priscilla, my secretary—she took Evie's place, you know—she let me know, and now they mention an ambulance. What the hell were you doing trying to shovel snow? . . ."

He held up a finger on his right hand and I took it to mean that I should shut up. I positioned a chair next to his bed, found my place, and listened.

Jesús might have been talking to me, or it might have been to someone else only he recognized. He drifted between delirium and lucidity.

"My job was to work ahead of the crew, planting the dynamite that opened new passages for the men to clear out. I

worked by myself most of the time. We were in the mine before the sun came up, and when we came out, it was always dark. I lived in blackness for years. The days I didn't work, I drank in a dark bar. The sun was a myth that the children talked about."

The memories that had been jarred from my father's brain were flooding out in Spanish so fast that I couldn't follow all of it. These could be the last words from him, but I didn't hear all of them; I didn't understand some of it. When I wandered from his weak monotone, Evangelina took his place. My father was deathly ill, I had more trouble with cops and clients than was appropriate at my age, and yet, it was Evangelina who twisted in my guts and knotted around my heart. Her memory joined me in my father's struggle.

"*There was a night—I was drunk. Why not? We had been playing cards. I remember how the edges of the cards turned black from the coal dust that we couldn't wash off, that dug into our skin and under our fingernails. A stranger played with us, a man as dark as the mine, who dressed in black and never laughed. We didn't know him, but we were Mexicans working for a gringo mine company. We didn't know who or what he was, so we let him play. He could have been a spy for the company. We had no reason to fear him. What could he do to us? What could anyone do to us? We lived our lives in darkness.*"

His guttural laugh was almost frightening. Evangelina tapped me on the shoulder. It was her signal that my father needed some help. I wiped his brow and propped his pillow. He nodded his gratitude.

"*You know I am not superstitious, Louie. I believe in God, of course. I know you do not, or at least you have doubts. It's a decision each one makes for himself. For me, it has meant some peace. When your mother died, for example. But believing in God means that one must also believe in the devil. Strange, no, how the reverse is not true? Someone can be-*

19

lieve in the devil and not have to believe in God."

In recent years, Jesús had dredged up more stories from his past—tales about his youth, my mother, his experiences in Mexico and the States. But they had always been quick and vague, more like general passages in a journal than detailed accounts. This one was different.

"We played for hours, but no one seemed to win. A great deal of money was bet, and piles of it moved around the table, but I remember, when the game ended, we could not recall anyone winning a hand. It was easy to blame it on the liquor. The stranger was gone before any of us, and we joked that he had taken all our money, without us even knowing it."

He laughed again, and again I didn't welcome the sound.

"I walked home with a man named Cleofas. We were not friends, only fellow workingmen. He told jokes and sang pieces of songs, some of which I recognized and some I didn't. It was pitch-black. There didn't seem to be any stars, and the moon had disappeared. We picked our way along the road more by instinct than anything else. It seemed colder than usual, too. At the place in the road where we had to part company, we shook hands. It was almost dawn, and in two hours we would have to go to work, so we expected to see each other in a short time. I turned in the direction of my shack, when the stranger appeared, out of nowhere, and called out our names. 'Oye, Jesús. Cleofas. One more game. One more bet.' "

I didn't know this story. Some of it had to come from my father's illness, and the rest from his years.

"Cleofas was eager, and he agreed readily. I hesitated, and the stranger's eyes sparkled and danced at my timidity. We sat in the dirt. The stranger produced a deck of cards. My head ached and I felt as if I were swimming underwater, but I played along. Cleofas bragged about his winnings during the night, and again the stranger's eyes exploded at us. We

20

knew Cleofas lied. The stranger asked, 'High card?' and Cleofas said, 'It's your deal, your game.' The stranger threw in a pile of greenbacks and coins. I didn't know how much, so I recklessly took out a wad of money from my jacket pocket and practically hurled it in the stranger's direction. 'The ace of spades is the death card. You lose automatically.' Cleofas spoke again. 'Whatever, man, just do it.' The stranger smiled as he shuffled the deck; then he dealt one card to each of us, and one to himself. There was a rush of wind. My eyes caught a handful of gravel. For a second or two, I couldn't see. When my eyes had stopped watering, Cleofas was holding his card, his face tight and his teeth clenched. It was the ace of spades—no surprise. The stranger's laughter competed with the moaning wind. He stood and showed his card—an ace of diamonds. I reached for my card, but Cleofas stopped me; he pressed my hand into the dirt. 'No, brother. It's not necessary. I've lost, and he's won. We should go now.' The stranger made a move to stop us, but a gust whirled the dirt and we were surrounded by a twister of rocks and sand. My card flew into the air. I caught a glimpse of it as it sailed to the stars. Cleofas grabbed me and we practically ran home. The money and the stranger were gone."

Jesús stopped and rested. He closed his eyes. His breathing was uneven. I looked for the buzzer to call a nurse.

"The next day, I overslept. I thought for sure I would be fired. I had drunk too much, and only vaguely remembered the poker game. I tried to think of an explanation for the boss, but I knew nothing I said would matter. I would have to leave the mine. But when I stopped at the supervisor's tent, no one noticed me. They were all busy with the accident, with the fire in the mine. I pitched in immediately. A group of us went into the mine, but there was nothing we could do. A man had been trapped in a cave-in, and then an explosion, a fire. The boss closed off that section of the hole, and he told us we had been lucky. Only one man had died, and he said my name, 'Jesús Montez.' But, as you must know, it had been Cleofas. He had covered for me when I was late—he took my place planting the explosives. And he had died."

His voice had grown weaker. I said, "That's enough, Dad. Rest now. I'll see you tomorrow."

I bent down and smoothed his scalp. His hand grabbed mine and pulled me close.

"I saw my card when it flew in the wind, Louie. It was the ace of spades. We both had been dealt the ace of spades."

He struggled to form the words. I leaned forward until I felt his mustache tickle my ear.

"You do what is right, Louie. In the fields, there may not be a reason for the way the crops have been planted, but there is always a source for the water. Sometimes the work is to find that source and forget about reasons. Call the kids. I want to see everyone. One more time."

My apprehension had been correct. I wasn't the right guy for this.

The surviving "kids" included four sons, two daughters, their respective spouses and exes, and I didn't know how many grandchildren. Not all of us were still around. And of the immediate family, I was the only one in Denver. Maria had died years ago, when I was a boy; Graciela would drive up from Albuquerque; Chuey would con something from Phoenix; Juanito would fly in from Sacramento; Carlos lived near Chicago, but I didn't know how to reach him; Roberta was in the state, up in Fort Collins, on a ranch with her husband and three children. It was my job to call them and tell them to get to Denver as soon as they could. The old man might not last the week.

Sleep intermittently teased his mind. Several minutes escaped the room before I whispered good-bye. In the darkness, I made quick plans to call all my relatives and to find out what this Dr. Webster was up to.

The bright hospital corridor did a number on my eyes, so it was a second or two before the lumbering object moving toward me registered. My vision was cleared by the rough hand on my shoulder, stopping me in my tracks as I tried to move around the guy who stood in my way.

"Don't race off, Montez. Let's catch up on old times."

Detective Ignacio Tenorio still used greasy kid stuff, and he insisted on wearing the ugliest-looking clothes a man can find in the bargain basements of department stores going out of business. His personality hadn't changed in the thirty years I had known him. When we first met, he was introduced as "Ug" Tenorio, and it was an apt description of his face. I learned, however, that his nickname came from the word in his vocabulary that he used repeatedly, in answer to almost any question, or as a response to almost any situation.

"Hey, Tenorio, want to drink some beer?"

"Ugh!"

"Want to cruise for girls?"

"Ugh!"

"Want to try living life?"

"Ugh!"

Ignacio Tenorio was an embarrassment to the neighborhood clique, and I suspected he became a cop in a feeble attempt to get even. We had clashed several times in the courtroom. I did my defense attorney gig, and he played the part of righteous peace officer nailing the perps and taking occasional jabs at the perps' counsel. He *had* busted some of his old homeboys over the years. I had to think I was next on his list, especially with the zealous way he locked his hand on my wrinkled suit jacket.

I wrenched free and we did incomplete pirouettes on the

gleaming hospital floor. I positioned myself against the wall and tried to maintain eye contact with Tenorio.

"Hey, Ignacio, my secretary said something about you dropping by. If it's about those parking tickets, I'm working on them. I've been kind of busy lately."

Tenorio smiled. He seemed to be enjoying himself.

"You've got explaining, Louie. Officer Strayhorn just too convenient, ey. Now that the DA and Internal Affairs are looking into Esch." He never had learned how to speak in complete sentences.

"What about Strayhorn? What are you talking about, man? Quit horsing me around. I've got to see the doctor about my father, call the family, I don't know what—"

"Sure. You play dumb. Okay. Strayhorn was killed, yesterday morning. The bribery charges about to blow up. And you're the one. The man who got to Strayhorn. For that piece of shit Esch. The sister must have been good. At least I hope she was, ey."

I had no clue as to what Tenorio was after, and it seemed risky to play along with the hope of finding out. I did the old "I won't answer questions until I talk with my lawyer" number. Tenorio tried to ease off and insisted that formally I wasn't a suspect, but he quickly retreated out of Denver General when I demanded having another mouthpiece around. He promised to get back to me, and when he did, he wouldn't be "as nice."

Hospitals and cops have always been a bad mix for me.

3

◆

D r. Webster wasn't available to talk with me. I wrote him a curt note and left it with Clara. He had my phone numbers and, I expected, a sense of my impatience.

I had borrowed one of Lisa's extra cars to get to the hospital. It was a svelte fast-backed two-seater, and I wasn't aware of all of its quirks. I got hung up in the gears, lost control on a couple of icy corners, and had a bad time crossing Speer to get to Zuni. Eventually, I landed in the driveway to my house. I stopped too quickly, the engine died, and it was possible that I smelled something burning.

I practically ran through a perfunctory shower. I scavenged the dryer for the shirt with the least wrinkled collar, then covered it with a sweater. With a double-breasted blue blazer, the overall effect wasn't too bad, but there was no way I was ready for work. I dug out my address book and found the phone numbers for my relatives, then hesitated. Maybe if I delayed telling them about Dad, I could also delay the resolution of his story. I rationalized, made excuses— avoided reality. Later, I would make the calls. There could be good news about the old man in the afternoon.

I felt as if I was at the end of a boozy night rather than at the beginning of another long day. I popped a can of beer and half of it was gone in two swallows. Evangelina's boogie to L.A. also meant the return in my life of a more prominent position for alcohol, not that it had been totally subdued. But at least when we lived together, I wasn't doing Bud for breakfast.

I reviewed the morning paper for the news I had missed during my interlude at Lisa's. Strayhorn's death had made the front page.

The article had been cleaned up, obviously, and there were only sparse details about how he died. Officially, Strayhorn had suffered an accident while on an investigative trip to the western slope. He was following up on the shooting of a mountain loner by a deputy sheriff. The loner was a suspect in a string of armed robberies across the state, including some in Denver. Strayhorn's car had taken a curve on Monarch Pass a hair too fast for the weather conditions. A search party found his mangled auto and just as mangled body covered in snow at the foot of a thousand-foot ravine.

He was a ten-year veteran with a trio of commendations, and recently he had been recognized by the mayor for his volunteer work at a local rec center. Standard stuff that could apply to almost any cop with more than two years on the force.

My work on the Esch case had turned up more interesting details about the enigmatic Officer Strayhorn.

Ambitious and smart, Strayhorn had garnered a series of quick promotions, but after five years, his climb had stopped abruptly. He was a cop who had bounced over the line a few times. His problems appeared to have origins in a drug case involving one of Denver's more obscure criminals—identified only as "Juju" in the file I'd seen. I remembered from old Tarzan movies that *juju* meant something about magic or power. Strayhorn had been "administratively disciplined" for an incident that I hadn't been able to get any details on, but it had to do with excessive force, a confession from Juju that got eighty-sixed by a judge, and some dark but elusive insinuations by a young lady friend of Mr. Juju. It was all hush-hush around the station, and I'd seen as much as I did only because the first prosecutor who talked to me about Esch's case was a young guy I originally mistook for one of the DA's student interns. The young eager beaver bragged about recently passing the bar exam, and that was good enough for me to squeeze as much as I could before somebody with more wear and tear stopped me.

He was replaced rather rapidly when Strayhorn complained to his DA buddies, a bit melodramatically, about what I was prying into. As it turned out, Strayhorn's mistake in the Esch case had been the linchpin of my motion.

There was a chance that I could lose the appeal, and then Jimmy and I actually would have to present a defense at a trial. Even to spaced-out Jimmy Esch, that must have sounded like piss floating in the wind. But Strayhorn's death certainly put a cramp in the DA's ongoing prosecution of Jimmy Esch.

I had to have a heart-to-heart with my client. Jimmy Esch had avoided me since the hearing on my motion to suppress. He was a busy man—that I understood. Maintaining a five-hundred-dollar-a-day habit must seem like a career. I wanted to believe that he could make time for the legal eagle who so far had kept his no-good butt out of the joint.

A phone call to Esch would have been futile. I opted for spontaneity and wrestled Lisa's car to Esch's apartment on Race Street. Jimmy lived near Manual High and his connections to the drugs that he needed more than money.

The decrepit building looked dangerously close to falling apart. I climbed the iced-over rickety stairs to his second-story flat. Although I tried to be as unobtrusive as possible, ominous-looking men and women stared as I made my way to his door. They leaned over the railing or unabashedly watched from windows. I had been to Jimmy's place, but always with him by my side, or waiting for me at the top of the stairs. Suddenly, my blazer and wing tips weren't a wise fashion choice. I realized that, although more expensive, my outfit was similar to Tenorio's when he had questioned me in the hospital corridor. I must have looked more cop than Dick Tracy.

I walked though the ajar door as though that's what I expected, and I shut it in the faces of Jimmy's neighbors with the right touch of bureaucratic rudeness. I had maybe five minutes before I had to deal with them again.

Before anything else, I noticed the smell. It was impossible not to. The odor was corporeal, almost heavy, and disgusting, and I didn't want to think about it.

A cold dampness hung in the air, and although I couldn't see it, I felt cloudy vapor roll out my nostrils with each breath. Soiled, torn curtains covered the windows. Strange diffuse shapes huddled in the corners. I clicked the light switch, but the darkness remained. My eyes played tricks with the contours of the room, and shadows seemed to move. I felt smothered. The smell was everywhere. I inched my way along the wall until I touched fabric. With a violent yank of my hand, I clumsily tore at a curtain. I jumped back when the clattering curtain rod bounced at my feet. I blew warmth on my fingers as I tried to slow down my forced breathing. I didn't want to take in too much of the room's air.

Sunlight from the streaked window incompletely exposed the trashed front room. Three wooden chairs and a kitchen table lay on their sides. The couch where I had talked with my client had its pillows missing, and yellow stuffing spread across the floor from a gash along the back.

A cellular phone leaned against a wooden crate. I tapped the buttons, but nothing happened. The crate was partially covered by scraps of paper with crude writing.

Muffled, agitated voices slipped under the front door. I suspected that the local chapter of the neighborhood watch was going to put a stop to my unwanted prying. I prepared to rap legal mumbo jumbo at them—hey, I *was* the occupant's lawyer—when my attention was distracted by Jimmy's shoes protruding from under a pile of trash bags in a corner of the filthy kitchen. The angle was all wrong. Splotches of dry blood had ruined my client's Nikes.

I didn't want to walk over to the terrible small mound. I forced my body to turn to it, and I almost had my nerve in control; I had almost decided to give Jimmy the respect of looking at him, certifying what had happened.

The door slammed opened with a loud whoosh, and before I did anything at all, pumped-up men swooped in around me, hollering and forcing me to the floor. Ignacio Tenorio's knees stabbed my back as he pressed my face into the sour carpet.

"You're under arrest, Montez. You have the right to remain silent; you have the right to an attorney . . ."

I didn't hear him finish Mirandizing me. I jerked my head upward and fixed my eyes on the other policemen, who went right to what I had stared at as they charged into the apartment. The smell made sense now. They dug out Jimmy's shoes and Jimmy's legs and the pieces of the rest of his body. The appeal of *The People of the State of Colorado* v. *James P. Esch* was unexpectedly moot.

I expected my lawyer, Ricardo Ybarra, to dash into the interrogation room at any moment, waving bail motions and habeas corpus orders, and yank me away from the clutches of Tenorio and Martinez. Jimmy's killing had affected me—

spooked the hell out of me—and maybe I'm my own worst client, but this time I didn't see any harm in talking with the Latino versions of Starsky and Hutch.

"I'll tell you everything I know, which is nothing. I don't know how or why Strayhorn was murdered, if that's what happened. I don't know how or why Jimmy was butchered. And for sure, I can't tell you anything about Lisa."

The two policemen had laid that last one on me after the initial processing was done and the three of us sat around a shaky card table, going along with the routine of Q&A, although none of us expected anything to come of it.

Tenorio played good cop—a stretch, but he showed flashes of talent.

"I understand, Louie. You hung with the wrong crowd, now defend them. Some of the shit has to stick. Maybe you got in a little too deep. I'll do what I can, if you help me out, ey."

On the other hand, Martinez loved the role of bad cop. He was the infuriated partner, the man who had every reason for wanting to beat my brains into gravy pulp. He had lost his longtime buddy. His case spiraled down the toilet because of the loophole I had stretched to cover the City and County Building. Now he had the chance to even up with the defense attorney who seemed to be at the root of it all.

Martinez had recently been promoted, and he obviously wanted to impress his mentor.

"We wanted to talk with Lisa Esch about the bribery charge against Strayhorn—and about her brother. But she's disappeared, and nobody seems to know where she is. I think you know where she is, Montez."

I didn't respond, but it didn't seem to matter. Martinez lit a cigarette while he thought of his next clever tack. His brain worked against the skin of his rather large forehead.

The room's air was stale and hot. I draped my blazer across the back of my chair. The confined space and the close attention I received from the two cops made me uncomfortable, claustrophobic. I thought about discarding my sweater, too, but Tenorio and Martinez stayed with their suit coats, and I didn't want to appear to be less ardent than they about the interrogation.

"You were with her last night, and the last one to see her alive today. Enough people saw you at the courthouse when she picked you up. We placed you at the Skyline. The bartender knows her. Remembers seeing her with a dark, short, paunchy Mexican in a suit and tie. Said he looked kind of like a lawyer. That's you, Montez. Paunchy—and kind of like a lawyer."

"And that's kind of humorous, Martinez. Almost as humorous as this charade. Think, man. Why would I want Strayhorn dead? You two bozos screwed up the search. You guys were my defense. I should have given Strayhorn a big kiss, not a shove over Monarch."

Martinez jumped from his chair, cocked his fist, and took aim. I waited for the punch.

On the one hand, I certainly didn't want the pain and hassle of a broken nose, but, on the other, it might be worth it for a quick settlement with the city. I can't help myself. It's my lawyer training.

He slammed the tabletop and kicked back his chair. Tenorio grabbed him and held him at bay. He delivered a quick speech, more for Martinez's benefit than mine. There went the lawsuit.

"Easy, boys. Montez, you know how this goes. Cut the bullshit. Answer our questions!"

I used a tone that I relied on when jurors scowled at my client during closing arguments.

"I *am* leveling with you guys. I haven't seen her since this morning. I borrowed her car. You found it parked in the street across from Esch's dump. I'm not hiding anything. I was looking for Jimmy to ask him what was up with Stray-

31

horn and why you were leaning on me about him. But I don't know what's going on. I wish I did."

Tenorio shook his head.

"Louie, Louie. *¡Cálmese!* Look from our perspective. The DA gets calls. Strayhorn into shit, about your case. He blew it. For money? *¿Quién sabe?* Then Jimmy. And you're there, man. Now the sister. Gone, vanished. And her place wrecked. Blood, too. Louie, blood all over the walls. Not good, ey?"

That shook me. The job on Jimmy had been vicious, sadistic. The poor kid had to have suffered. I tried not to think about Lisa in the same way.

"Tell me something, Tenorio."

"What, ey?"

"You know what happens when somebody tells you not to think about elephants?"

"What the fuck are you jabbering about?"

"I'll wait for my lawyer, gentlemen. Until then, I could definitely use a cup of coffee."

4

$\blacklozenge$

My arrest had been a formality more than anything else. They had to do something with me. They *had* bagged me at the scene of a murder, under suspicious circumstances. Tenorio intended to recommend to the DA that I be charged with bribery, bribing a witness, and obstructing government operations. The bribery offenses were class-three and class-four felonies that carried sentences of four to sixteen and two to eight years. A conviction on any of the charges would mean disbarment. And that was before Tenorio dug into the big stuff—at least one murder, one very suspicious fatal accident, and a probable abduction that, given the odds, had also ended in death.

Fortunately, they didn't quite have enough, yet, for the felony complaint. They knew Jimmy was dead when I arrived. They were watching his apartment and saw my uneasy sprint up the stairs to his place. The initial reports on the postmortem body changes had concluded that Jimmy's murder had taken place sometime after midnight. Lisa was my alibi, if she was still alive. Tenorio didn't want to overplay his hand. The tension was audible in his voice—he wanted me, but he had to take his time. He wasn't about to screw up his chance finally to nail me.

Without a formal charge, Ybarra didn't have any problem whisking me away from their clutches. The cops impounded Lisa's car, so Ybarra drove me to his office. Then we talked; that is, he talked. I didn't know anything, as I tried to tell Tenorio and Martinez. Ricardo Ybarra, on the other hand, had learned a great deal in a short amount of time about what the cops thought about me and the rest of the cast of *The People of the State of Colorado* v. *James P. Esch.*

We sat in his comfortable digs near Larimer Square. Subdued light from a pair of brass desk lamps cast halos around the leather chairs where he practiced the arts of interviewing and client wooing. There was an outdoor feel to the room—dark wood paneling, a painting of a fly fisherman casting on a mountain stream, and Ricardo dressed in a heavy tweed jacket and cowboy boots. The man recognized the importance of flaunting his success.

Ybarra had a very good business. He and his four partners prided themselves on being *the* small firm that could manhandle any prosecutor, opposing counsel, or judge. They had a thriving criminal-defense, domestic, and commercial-litigation practice, mixed in with the right attitude about office parties, a droll appreciation for the offbeat, and a talent for attracting the best clients—victims with more than adequate resources to finance a good legal fight.

He had a degree from Stanford, and he'd drifted into Colorado almost as an afterthought. I hadn't known him until the morning he entered his appearance on behalf of one of several codefendants in a case where I also sat at defense counsel's table. At that time, he was cutting his trial attorney's teeth with the public defender's office. I saw him fairly regularly after that in the courtroom, briskly manipulating the two dozen or so cases he picked up at morning arraignments, and I was impressed.

I had never met a Yaqui, but, because I didn't know any better, I concluded that Ybarra's family must have roots in that tribe. He was darker than I and just as short, with a pockmarked face. But his distinguishing feature was his prominent nose, centered beneath craggy eyebrows.

I occasionally called him for assistance with a tricky defense, and, once or twice, to help me out of my own jams. The Esch case was the stickiest yet.

"Here's what I've got, Louie. Internal Affairs instigated an investigation of Strayhorn almost the day you got your decision from Bernstein. You should appreciate that Martinez is the man who turned them on. He didn't know why Strayhorn testified the way he did. As far as he knew, Strayhorn *had* felt an object in your client's drug bag. He had every reason to search it for weapons. But when his partner went belly-up in court, well, that rang his chimes, and he talked to the wrong people about his suspicions. At least wrong from your point of view."

"Martinez? Hey, he was all over me about Strayhorn. I got the impression he blamed me for leading the guy astray."

"He will stand by him, you know that. But Strayhorn'd been a smudge on the department for years. He goes . . . uh, that is, he used to go too far with defendants, and sometimes witnesses. And he'd been accused of being on the take before. The department never found enough to dump him. Martinez might even have been working for Internal Affairs. They weren't known as close partners."

"So the cops think Strayhorn threw the case—for what? Some of Esch's money?" The implications riled me. "And they think I was the guy who set it up? Oh, man! I won that case with hard work. I never talked to Strayhorn about reworking his testimony. I didn't have to. I didn't need to sub-orn perjury, for Christ's sake! Strayhorn gave up his story early on. The DA just didn't think I would know what to do with it. Damn. Damn!"

"But now it's more critical, Louie. Strayhorn and Esch are dead. And you benefit from their untimely deaths. According to the DA, Esch and Strayhorn are probably the only ones who knew the details about the bribe. . . ."

"Hey, there wasn't any fucking bribe. . . ."

"If there was one. Easy—you have to know what's coming down, Louie. You're about to be fried, man. The way the DA figures, the heat was on Strayhorn. He was beginning to crack. A friend on the force told me that he had more or less admitted that something off-kilter had happened to the Esch case. It was only a matter of time before he gave up his coconspirators—you and Jimmy Esch."

"And a day or two later, Strayhorn takes a dive off of Monarch Pass and Jimmy's laid out, disemboweled."

"The sister, too. She vanishes just when you need her. She may be the only one who can keep you out of Tenorio's mitts, the only one who can clear your involvement with her brother's killing. You better pray she doesn't turn up dead, Louie."

We quickly worked out the details of his representation. It was all very professional, very stylish. He was expensive, and, colleague or not, he expected a retainer that put a massive dent in my checking account. We made arrangements based on the installment plan. And because I was without a car, I had to catch a cab to my office. *Esch* was turning out to be a very costly case.

Getting busted helped put my personal life in perspective. Evangelina's ghost had disappeared while I sparred with Tenorio and Martinez, and my lawyer's tough talk convinced me that I had more pressing priorities than a little old broken heart. Lisa worked on me, too. However brief our relationship had been, I had to admit that the woman had managed to ignite some embers that Evangelina had doused with ice water. More than that, though, was a nagging pang that I owed her, that she wouldn't have ended up where she had—wherever that was—if she hadn't spent time with me, and that we were all tied together in a ball of knotty complications that centered on her dead brother.

Finally, there was Jesús. The most important obligations I had were spending time with him, making sure he was going to be all right, and gathering his family around to lend their support. It was the only piece of my life that Jimmy Esch hadn't yet contaminated.

The afternoon was about over by the time I walked into my office. Priscilla was a wreck. She was under siege. The phone was ringing; she clutched a wrinkled bundle of message slips; a delivery man was trying to dump a package on her desk, but she wouldn't sign for it; and a pair of angry elderly women were demanding to see the *abogado*. Priscilla had at least one saving grace. She spoke Spanish fluently. Her bilingual expertise was the main reason I had hired her. Her skill and patience had been put to the ultimate test by the Alvarado sisters. My secretary couldn't wait to turn them loose on me.

"Mr. Montez! I'm so glad you made it."

The sarcasm was thick, and she narrowed her eyes to let me know I would have to pay for deserting her without so much as a phone call. The two women turned as one and advanced on me. I tried to duck into my office, but they cornered me. They had dressed magnificently for their visit to my office—black hats with veils, gloves, long coats, colorful scarves, dress shoes, and their best dresses. Obviously, they had a very important legal problem that required immediate attention.

"Señor Montez. We have been waiting for you! We must see you. It is a matter of extreme urgency."

Carmelita Alvarado, the younger, spoke better English than Manuelita, and she assumed the leadership role whenever the two spinsters had to deal with the world outside their backyard garden.

"Ah, yes, ladies. How are you? Please have a seat, a cup of coffee. I'll be with you in a few minutes. Priscilla, can you please get them something to drink?" But they wouldn't be put off so easily.

Manuelita, being the elder, had the responsibility of explaining the problem, in Spanish.

"It's the Borrego boy, again! Oh, that little monster. And I love children! But him, that Bobby, that creature from hell. If you don't stop him, we will defend ourselves! I know how to use the rifle, if I have to!"

They had been fighting with the neighbor's eight-year-old son for almost a year. I had talked with the parents and they had politely told me and the sisters to mind our own loony business. Their son, according to the indignant Borregos, had nothing to do with the dotty old maids—they were busybodies, mean old ladies, and everything else they could throw at me during our brief five-minute telephone conversation. But the kid had stayed away from my clients, and I had not been called by Carmelita and Manuelita in months.

Priscilla had extricated herself from the phone and the package man, and she served a cup of tea for Manuelita and a diet soda for Carmelita. Her intercession gave me a chance to retreat into my office with the stack of phone messages in my hands. I promised the women that I would counsel them in a mere ten minutes.

There were the usual vollies from three or four other attorneys with whom I was playing the latest round of phone tag. Nothing from Lisa or the hospital. David Padgett had called to belatedly congratulate me on the Esch decision. That was one referral that demanded a personal note of thanks from me. At the bottom of the batch were messages from most of my brothers and sisters. Somehow, they had already found out about Dad. In my eye, the notes were curt and accusatory.

"On our way to Denver. Wish you had called us as soon as Dad got sick."

"Please call. What's going on with Dad?"

"Will get there as soon as I can. How bad is it?"

And finally, there was the one message I hadn't wanted, but the one that had to be waiting.

"You should have called to tell me about Dad. Why did I have to find out from Graciela? Where the hell are you? I'll be in town tonight. Meet me at the hospital. What's wrong with you, Louie?"

At the end of the message, Priscilla had scribbled "Chuy?" Almost. Aside from my father, Jesús Montez, Jr., had been the most dominant male figure of my childhood. I couldn't remember ever using his given name. He had always been Chuey; he would always be Chuey. He would always be the guy who had bullied and tormented me as a child, and who still hadn't let up. I cursed and breathed deeply before I told Priscilla to bring in the Alvarado sisters.

Gathering the family added a nice touch to everything else that had gone right with life lately.

I assuaged the sisters and promised to call the Borregos. I talked on the phone with other clients and did what I could to make amends with Priscilla. But my heart wasn't in it. I had to admit that I didn't care enough about Priscilla to worry about whether she would quit now that her boss was a suspect in a murder and she had seen what kind of business dropped into my office on a fairly regular basis. Lisa had been my rebound catch in the sack, and Priscilla had fulfilled the same role in my office, without the sex. I wouldn't have noticed when she left for the day, but I had to ask to borrow her car. She grudgingly agreed.

I jumped back into the Esch case, the case that wouldn't end, as I flipped through one of the many files.

There was a time when Judge Hector Garcia might have helped me, but he was gone. I didn't know anybody on the police force well enough to trust, or compromise, certainly not with Strayhorn's death still making headlines. I couldn't involve Ybarra more than he already was—I needed him as my lawyer, and for that I had to protect him. I'd keep him out of the places where I thought I would cruise, as well as avoid telling him all the tawdry things I counted on uncovering in my own investigation. Ybarra was my mouthpiece, not my hound dog.

I shut the manila folder and tried to stuff it back into the expanding file with the rest of the papers in the case. A photograph fell on my desk. It was a mug shot—a picture of Jimmy's codefendant, Alton Enoch. The black man smiled at the camera, but I wasn't reassured. The rest of his face scowled, clearly broadcasting the message that it was a big mistake to mess with him, even if you were a cop.

I looked through the witness file. Enoch's name and address were on the endorsement list filed by the DA. The address was near City Park, not too far from Jimmy's apartment. I had time for a visit before I thought I should meet the family at the hospital.

The weather had eased up and a break appeared imminent. There had been an increase in the temperature to near the freezing mark, which usually meant that the next day would be even warmer. Slush and muddy water would flow in the streets. It was the first good thing I could say about the day.

5

In the fading twilight, hidden but threatening to be more than a trace in the air soon, spring waited. The cold days of January had a hint of more sunlight than the cold, depressing days of December. Even so, I was in darkness by the time I navigated Priscilla's Chevy through Alton Enoch's Eastside neighborhood, craning my neck for a house number or a street sign. Twice around the same block and eventually I found what I thought was Enoch's house. By illegally parking head-on, I confirmed the address with my headlights.

A nimbus of yellow light radiated from a large picture window and bounced off the ice and snow that framed the porch. The house looked like any other on the block— old, worn-out, and abused by too many temporary dwellers. Funny—that's when Evangelina sauntered into my thoughts, and for a whacked-out flash, I was lonely and nostalgic and worthless.

I sat in the rapidly cooling car and stared at the house for several minutes. I didn't know what I watched for; maybe I wanted something to happen that would convince me that my gut feeling was right—that this was a really bad idea. But it was part of the plan—it had to be—I just didn't understand the plan.

I had uncovered enough background on Alton Enoch to make me pause and actively ponder the consequences of my unannounced visit. He was an ex-con with a penchant for games of chance that routinely ended in violent disagreements. As was the case with too many of my male clients, drugs and women had played key roles in the development of his crime history. There was an added bonus with Enoch—a seamless blend between his psychotic mentality and his distinctive, volatile disposition. He once had sliced off a pair of his cousin's toes because the man had made a disparaging remark about the color of a lady friend's shoes. I promised myself to refrain from fashion comments.

I swallowed my anxiety in a deep breath of cold air and marched up the icy sidewalk. Loud arguing greeted me.

"Motherfucker, you fucking motherfucker!"

"Shut up, bitch, before I fuck you up worse than you already are!"

I stood half in darkness and half on the edge of the light from the window. I stalled for a second, knocked on the weather-beaten door, and remembered to breathe at a regular rate. The voices stopped immediately. I knocked again, a bit louder.

The door jerked open and Enoch peered through the night and wintry haze of the porch. He held a glass of dark liquid. His torso swayed in the doorway. It must have been difficult for him to see me. My neck craned upward as I looked into yellow rheumy eyes and a malignant face.

"What the fuck you want?"

"I'm Luis Montez, Jimmy Esch's lawyer. We've never met, Mr. Enoch, but I've talked with your lawyer—about the coke bust in your car. I wanted to ask—"

"Jimmy Esch! Ain't that a bitch." His hoarse, dull voice slurred the words. "You don't have a client, mister. His case is closed, man. Good riddance! What the fuck you want?"

It was a simple question, but I didn't know what I wanted, so I hesitated with my answer just long enough to agitate Enoch. He took a step in my direction. Drops of the dark liquid swished out of his glass and spotted his multi-colored sweater.

The woman hollered at Alton's back.

"What the hell you doing? Shut the fucking door; I'm freezing my ass off!"

Alton didn't seem to have time for her. Again he asked, "What the fuck you want?"

"Look, man, it's about Esch, and Strayhorn, and *your* fucking case." The colorful language had rubbed off on me. "There's all kinds of fucking shit going on with the cops, and Jimmy, and his sister, and I'm getting squeezed in the middle. I thought you could help me out, that's all."

The woman appeared behind Enoch and glared at me from around his shoulders. She was almost as tall as Enoch. She wrapped her arms around his waist and rubbed parts of his body that would respond to such rubbing. Apparently, she had forgotten about their earlier tiff.

Enoch did his best to ignore her.

"I can't help myself, much less the lawyer of a dead white boy that almost got me sent up. You should go back wherever it is you came from, lawyer. I ain't got nothing for you."

"Maybe you do. You don't know until you hear me out. It could mean something to me that you can't even guess at. It might even help you and Glory Jane Jacquez with the charges still hanging over your heads."

Glory Jane's name drew an immediate response from Alton and the woman.

He hurriedly looked over his shoulder. She grabbed a

43

handful of his sweater, pinching and twisting. She yelled, at no one in particular. "That bitch, that whore! I knew it. I knew it! Damn you, Alton. . . ."

Alton grimaced from the woman's grip on his belly. Then he smiled.

"I can't talk to you now, man. I'll call, tomorrow. . . . Ow, ouch! Damn, Rochelle, stop it!"

She dragged him back into the house, turning and kneading the front of his stomach. But before Alton finished his abrupt exit, I had balanced a business card between his long, shiny blue-black fingers. He smiled one more time, just before the door slammed in my face.

Rochelle screamed at Alton. "I'm going to stop this crap! You and that Mexican hole! If you know how, better start praying, motherfucker."

"Baby, baby. Relax. It ain't what you think."

Alton convinced me, and I had a hunch he could convince Rochelle, too.

The drive across downtown to the hospital provided the time to try to arrange the pieces. There were other people I had to talk to about Jimmy Esch. Alton Enoch was a good beginning, if he actually followed through and called me. Glory Jane Jacquez meant something to him, obviously much more than Jimmy had. She represented a link between Jimmy and Alton that I had to figure out, and to do that, I would have to find her, too.

As I turned from Eighteenth onto Broadway and headed south to Denver General, I had to laugh. The Esch case had landed in my lap as a favor. Dave Padgett had sent me Jimmy Esch on a rush basis. Padgett didn't do criminal defense work and his office had some kind of a conflict of interest, but he had promised the Esch family that he would find a substitute attorney. He had admitted that he had tried another lawyer before me, the famous Arnold Mansfield, but it was too much of a scheduling problem for the first choice. He had pleaded with me to interview Esch and at least get the ball rolling on his defense. Finally, he had stated the obvious—Beatrice and Greg Esch were very important clients to his firm.

"You understand, Louie. If it looks like I helped out their brain-dead son, they'll keep throwing business our way, and you get a nice retainer. What do you say?"

I had known what had to be done with the preliminary matters in the case, and I had to acknowledge that I owed Padgett a favor or two. The well-known Esch family wealth also helped. I reasoned that at least I wouldn't have to fret about timely payment of my fee.

"Okay, Padgett, tell the family you found the man for their boy."

My pinch hit now threatened to land me somewhere in the state prison system, stripped of my license to practice law and everything else that still meant anything to me. And I hadn't yet received the last installment on my fee from Ma and Pa Esch.

Down Broadway, across Colfax Avenue, beyond the gold-capped Capitol shining in the night light of Denver, then right on Eighth, I repeated to myself, You'd think I'd learn. You'd think I'd learn.

It wasn't critical, but as long as I was trying to tie up the bundle of loose ends, I added Dave Padgett to my list.

The heater in Priscilla's car quit. The fan stopped humming, no heat circulated, and a subtle numbness crept into my fingers.

By the time I parked in the hospital lot, I vainly tried to force a semblance of heat into my feet by stomping them on the floor of the car. A lone policeman stood outside the wide swinging doors of the entrance, blowing on his glove-covered hands as though it made a difference. He nodded at me as I passed, and I said, "I hate winter." He nodded again.

My family had turned the third floor of Denver General

45

into a campground. Assorted nephews and nieces slept on the floor in the waiting room, in the chairs, and up against the wall. Discarded and empty potato chip bags and crumpled candy bar wrappers littered the room and the hallway. My brothers Juanito and Chuey and sisters Graciela and Roberta were crowded into Dad's room, shoulder-to-shoulder, watching him, listening to another of his stories. Graciela approached slowly. She held out her arms and hugged me. I smelled liquor. The others gathered around us, and I was greeted with an overwhelming array of hugs and handshakes. My nephew Michael warmly offered to do whatever he could for my father.

Jesús grunted for my attention.

"Say, Dad. Doing better?"

He made a sign with his hands that implied he couldn't speak above a whisper. I bent down to him, as I had on my last visit.

He quietly told me, in a clear, steady voice, "It's too damn crowded in here, Louie. They're sucking up the air. I can't see the TV, and the kids are bawling all the time. Damn, Louie, help me out."

The old man might make it yet.

I turned to the relatives and, with a sweep of my arms, gathered them all as one, and then slowly, diplomatically, I herded them out of the room. We milled about the hallway, a small mob of pensive siblings, unsure about the future, mired in past regrets and animosities. They focused their concern, fear, and misgivings on me. One after another peppered me with questions and accusations. Nurses and an occasional doctor walked around us, some with disapproving glares, others with businesslike acceptance.

The relatives wanted me to tell them that Dad would be all right, that they could go back to wherever it was they had come from, and that I would fix it, the way I had always fixed the family problems. I was the damn lawyer, the one son who made real money, the one who understood institutions, bureaucracies, and the way to get things done. And if I couldn't, then what good was I, what good was my degree, my license?

I needed a drink.

I told them what I had learned from Clara, the nurse. I still hadn't spoken with Dr. Webster, but I assured everyone that I would see him soon, that we all would see him and hear the scoop on our father from the horse's mouth.

I was interrupted by a shrill holler from up the corridor. A boy with a vaguely familiar face crashed from the waiting room and charged down the hallway. His arms flailed the air, and his feet were on the verge of flying out from under him.

"It's Uncle Louie! On TV! On the news! Uncle Louie! Come and see!"

My brothers and sisters threw worried looks at me. They wanted an explanation. I said, "Now what?" and ran to the waiting room, where the TV had been hypnotizing the children.

My law school photograph shared the screen with Beatrice and Greg Esch. They were in an interview with Wanda Higgins, a short blond reporter who liked to camp out at the courthouse. Her forte was the ugly messes some lawyers and judges couldn't seem to avoid.

On my side of the screen, I grinned crookedly, obviously high, my long hair bunched up around my shoulders, draped across the peasant shirt all the politically conscious Chicano law students had decided to wear for the class pictures. On the other half of the screen, Mrs. Esch strained to keep her voice under control. Mr. Esch hugged her shoulders, nodding his head in approval, or shaking it in disgust.

"We trusted this man with our boy's future, with his life! And our daughter got involved with him, too. He took advantage of his position—he was our lawyer. He was supposed to

47

help Jimmy. But he bribed the policeman to change his testimony. In a million years, we didn't expect that. We didn't want that. All we wanted was a good lawyer who would do a decent job for Jimmy."

Higgins interjected, very smoothly, I thought. "The policeman allegedly bribed was Officer Strayhorn, the man found dead yesterday in a terrible mountain accident?"

"That's what we've been told. The police haven't come right out and charged him, but we know Luis Montez is responsible for the death of our son, and this policeman's, too. That's what we think, right, Greg?"

That last installment on my fee didn't look too secure.

The reporter tried to cap the segment, but she had a tough time retrieving the microphone from Mrs. Esch. The interview ended with a plea from Beatrice Esch.

"We're only asking that he tell us where Lisa is, where we can find our dear daughter. Please, please! How can anyone want to hurt an innocent girl? How can anyone be so cruel?" She broke down completely.

Higgins added that there had been no official statement from the district attorney's office other than to say that the prosecutors were waiting for results from forensics. She wrapped up her report as Mrs. Esch cried hysterically in the background. Tears streamed down the face of Mr. Esch.

Except for the continuing babble of the newscast, a nervous silence settled over the waiting room. Even the children were quiet as their mothers drew them close. Juanito played with a set of keys and kept his eyes off me. Chuey smirked in a corner of the room. Graciela and Roberta stared at their lawyer brother, now infamous, now a large blot on the Montez family's reputation. Not too many of us had ever been featured on the late-night news.

"So, where's everyone staying?" I asked.

6

Unexpectedly, Chuey suggested crashing at my house, and Michael didn't seem to care one way or the other. It made sense to everyone that the men without families, without women, should move in with me. Chuey had married only once, but there had been several women in his life. Now, he lived more or less alone, and Michael had rushed to his grandfather's sickbed without Inez or the kids. They waited in the San Luis Valley for word about whether they, too, would have to come to the city.

I had been alone since Evangelina flew my coop. My sons, Bernardo and Eric, had moved with their mother to her new home in Golden. They rarely had time to visit, and we talked most of the time by telephone. They respected their grandfather, and worried about him, but Gloria kept them in Golden. She had told me to call whenever I thought it would be good for the boys to visit. That meant they weren't going to camp out in the hospital with their cousins, or with me. That phone call was one I didn't want to make.

The rest of the family took over Dad's small home on the Westside, or rented a group of rooms at a motel not too far from the hospital, on South Broadway. That way, the bulk of Dad's visitors were near, just in case. I also suspected that no one wanted to be around Chuey and me. Our years of arguing had worn out most of them, and they didn't appreciate more rounds of bickering while Jesús slipped in and out of consciousness.

I looked in on Dad before I left with my new roommates. We were alone, and I didn't want to bother him. He was awake and he motioned for me to come to his side. The TV was turned on to Higgins's station. He had seen the same report the rest of us had watched.

Jesús could not move. He was barely breathing, and I wasn't sure he could talk. I didn't understand all the words.

"Cada quien puede hacer de sus calzones un papalote."

Something about pants and kites. *Santo Niño,* Dad, why do you do that to me?

Chuey had flown in, and Michael had loaned his pickup to his mother, Graciela. They had to rely on me for transportation, so they listened to the radio and talked, almost casually, about Jesús, the relatives, even the Broncos— anything to avoid my recent newsworthiness. During the drive to my house, I promised Chuey and Michael a beer.

I stopped at the Dark Knight Lounge, my secluded, moody haven that offered the only hope for isolation. Where had the reporters been when I had won the Esch motion to suppress? Now they wanted a quote, a reaction, from me, I was sure. A murdered son and a frantic mother can do that. But I really wasn't surprised that Mrs. Esch's histrionics had more public interest than a judge's decision to turn loose a dope dealer because of a lawyer's technicality.

Michael relaxed and took his time with his beer. The scorpion-shaped scar across his eyebrow changed color with each drink until it settled on a hue somewhere between brown and dark red.

Chuey noisily eased his mind by choking down beer, his eyes surveying the unknown bar. When he apparently was reassured, the muscles in his upper arms relaxed, and the grin that had tormented me for years returned.

Chuey had a bad case of an old Chicano illness. For as long as I could remember, he had accused me of showing off, pretending to be what I couldn't ever hope to be, of not being enough. I had always blamed his attitude on his obvious resentment of whatever success I had enjoyed. Some people called our disease *envidia.*

"Same old Little Louie. What was that all about, on the TV? If Dad sees that, it *will* kill him."

"Don't start on me, Chuey. That crap on the news is nothing."

"Nothing? Nothing, as in *nada?* I don't think so, Little Louie. Murder and kidnapping and a dead cop. Even I ain't ever been in that kind of nothing. Same old *cagada.*"

I reached across the table and grabbed his shirt. Michael coughed on his beer and tried to pry my hand off my brother's throat. Chuey glared at me, but he didn't move. We had been through this before. Sometimes it ended with insincere chuckles, both of us turning our backs and walking away, and sometimes it ended only when one of us drew blood.

"I said, don't start. I got enough to deal with without your bullshit. If it wasn't for Dad, I'd . . ."

"Don't weasel out of anything on Dad's back. And take your damn hands off me!"

He wrenched my wrist, but I refused to let go. He stood, and I stood with him. He strained against my grip, and I held on because I didn't know what would happen if I turned him loose. We twisted and turned in the booth, with Michael in the middle, vainly hollering for us to stop. Chuey cussed at me and I cussed back. He accused me of causing Dad's attack, whatever it was, and I reminded him that he hadn't visited the old man in months.

51

Michael squirmed out of the booth, out of the way. The bartender watched from the bar, his hand near something that he relied on when his customers crossed the line.

Chuey finally had enough of our dance. He slapped at my hand, tried to jerk free from my sweaty fingers, and knocked over his beer. Instantly, it flooded the table and flowed onto our shoes. In reflex, I released my hold and jumped back to avoid the dripping beer.

"Damn, man. Look what you did!"

Michael scrambled away and almost immediately returned with a bar rag. He wiped up the mess, holding back his amusement with muffled spasms. Chuey and I stared at each other, remembering the old arguments and taunts, trying to put this one into its right place.

Michael finally blurted, "You two—Christ! Same old Louie and Chuey. Try to cool it, at least for your father! Like kids, just like damn kids!"

The scene got the better of him, and he stood back from us, trying to lose himself in forced laughter.

Chuey and I shuffled, hemmed and hawed, a duo of impatient idiots, not sure if Michael was crazy or fed up, or maybe both. We knew he was right. And because we knew that, and the man we admired more than anyone else lay near death, and it was late and we were tired, and we were without a mother to talk to, and because we were afraid, we laughed, too, and our laughter was close to crying.

I made it to the office by 7:30, the best I could accomplish after the late night at the hospital and my amiable reunion with my older brother. I didn't want to wake Chuey, so I skipped breakfast. I didn't even fix any coffee.

The animals stalked and hovered in the dawn's early light. A van with a transmitter dish straddled the driveway of the building's parking lot, and two reporters stood at opposite ends of the front walk, earnestly talking into cameras for the morning news. When I pulled into the side alley off of Thirty-eighth and parked the car with the hope that I could sneak into the back, Wanda Higgins scurried from a company station wagon, microphone in hand, her cameraman wildly trying to keep up with her, both of them slipping in the slush.

I could have run into the office and tried to slam the door in Higgins's face, but that probably would not have helped my image. I strolled to the back door, trying to remember that I was innocent—I hadn't done anything to anybody, not recently, anyway, and I was just as shook up about Jimmy's killing as anybody else, almost. I was Luis Montez, Esq., ace attorney for the underdog.

Higgins thrust her microphone in my face, grazing my chin, and began to talk to me. She was as bright-eyed as she could pretend to be in the semidarkness of the end of winter, surrounded by lingering ice and snow, her words a foggy presence between us.

"Mr. Montez, do you have anything to say about the accusations made by Beatrice Esch that you are responsible for the death of her son, James, and the disappearance of her daughter, Lisa?"

I looked *suave,* I knew. I had on my best dark blue suit, a bright multicolored geometric tie, my black cashmere-blend topcoat, and a pair of killer sunglasses. I gave the cameraman a chance to focus on me. First impressions are the key, man, and I needed several thousand good ones from the morning news audience.

"I sympathize with Mrs. Esch's loss, naturally. And remember that I knew James Esch—he was my client. His death was tragic and horrible. He was a young man trying to turn the corner of his troubled life." Tenorio would gag on that, I thought. "But I can assure you, Ms. Higgins, and everyone else watching this"—I stared into the camera and conjured up a ton of sincerity—"I had absolutely nothing to

53

do with Mr. Esch's murder, or the disappearance of Ms. Esch."

That should have done it. I tried to squeeze past Higgins and her cameraman, but she stood her ground. She waved her microphone at me and I put my hands up to ward off her negligent use of the instrument. A hollow ache from the agitations of her first question had worked itself from my chin into my teeth.

"Mr. Montez, how about the rumors that you and Lisa Esch were having an affair?"

"Please, Higgins, get a grip. I'm not going to answer that kind of question."

I didn't like where the interview was heading. I pushed past her, but she outflanked me and caught me just as I opened the door.

"And what about James's share of his trust? The millions he was entitled to get one day. Beatrice Esch accused you of trying to get James Esch to challenge the terms of the trust, and she said that you were after your own cut of the Esch estate. What about that, Montez?"

That froze me, colder than the sudden gust that whipped my pretty tie and frazzled Higgins's carefully arranged hairdo. Trust? Estate? Millions?

More reporters, TV equipment, and cameramen scurried to us from the front of my office. They shouted, growled, and barked, demanding their share of the nefarious Luis Montez. My mouth rolled out the first words that popped into my bewildered and caffeine-deprived brain.

"What the fuck . . ."

So much for first impressions.

David R. Padgett did his best to make me comfortable. The door to his office was discreetly closed, he had ordered the receptionist to hold his calls, and two cups of fresh coffee sat on the round polished table between us. The firm's name wrapped around the blue mugs in gold lettering. He ceremoniously dumped a shot of expensive cognac in each cup, and I have to admit that the overall effect was good.

"God, Louie. What can I say? I can't believe how this thing has blown up. And I want it clear between us that I don't buy any of the accusations made by the Eschs or the cops. I've known you too long for that. I had nothing to do with that circus on the news. If there's anything I can do, you know I will. . . . What is there? What can I do?"

I had stormed into his office after my encounter with reporter Higgins. Although I was unexpected and intruding on a meeting he had scheduled with an associate in the firm, he had accommodated me with a hastily arranged conference and profuse apologies.

"Level with me, Dave. What's going on with the Eschs? What do you know about all this?"

He clutched his cup near his chest, then stood. He leaned against a bookcase while he fingered the spines of law books and treatises that had nothing to do with the way he practiced law. A high-tech, sinful-looking sound system clung to the wall, and I noticed a few CDs strewn about with planned randomness.

Dave Padgett was a handsome man, in an Anglo kind of way. The right touch of extra belly, now that he was past forty, and a classic, clean-cut, almost boyish face blended together well on a stocky, solid frame. He took too long to answer my question.

"Come on, Dave. I've been smeared across this state, my business ruined, just a nose hair from an indictment for murder, bribery, kidnapping—hell. Your clients have wrecked my life, and I can't get anything from you? Let's get real for a minute."

Padgett turned to me at the hint of a threat in my words. "Louie, please." His words had an edge that disappeared as quickly as it had tinged his voice. "I'm trying to think this through. I want to let you in on everything, but Beatrice and Greg are my clients. There are some things I can't talk about, you know that. I'm privy to confidences of theirs that even under subpoena I wouldn't divulge. It's the law for every lawyer, even you."

I wasn't sure if he was including me in his club grudgingly or if he wanted merely to underscore the obligation imposed on us by the rules of ethical behavior.

"Padgett, I'm in so much trouble that I really don't care to hear any lawyer palaver. I need to know what's going on."

"Let's try this. What *do* you know—what steps have you taken?"

"Hell, I haven't had time to do much of anything. I got hassled by Detective Tenorio. He's the one who told me that Strayhorn had bought it up on Monarch Pass. I tried to find Jimmy and, unfortunately, I did—too late. I've been arrested, and been the subject of one of Wanda Higgins's ream jobs. I thought I might learn what I could from Jimmy's pals, Alton Enoch and his girlfriend. Alton was . . . uh, too busy to talk with me, although he may still come around, and I have no idea where Glory Jane Jacquez is. I plan to keep looking for her. That's it. Now you. Your turn. What do you know?"

I could tell that he was thinking over my question. He returned to the table and carefully centered the ceramic mug on one of the firm's designer coasters.

"Okay, Louie. You're entitled to as much as I can tell you."

I waited.

"None of this had any relevance to your defense of Jimmy. There wasn't any need to tell you about these details. Believe me, Louie, I didn't mislead you or keep information from you that had anything to do with the charges against Jimmy."

"Okay, Dave. You're covered. I'm not accusing you. I

simply don't want to be in the dark anymore, especially if the Eschs are going to keep up with their media tirades."

He nodded his head solemnly—his way of letting me know he agreed with me.

"Beatrice and Greg Esch have been clients of the firm for years. We've handled almost all of their business transactions, defended against the litigation that always lands on people like them, and taken care of whatever legal bits and pieces they've had over the years. Everything from quieting title on empty lots they bought on spec, to changing their wills every two, three years, to setting up the financial futures of their children."

An intemperate, acid taste filled my mouth and I realized the mistake of coffee and cognac before lunch—hell, before breakfast. I pushed the cup away, almost burping as I tried to get him to keep talking.

"The trust that I've lately come to know about," I said.

"Sure, the trusts, and other items. These people have incredible amounts of wealth, socked away in real estate, mutual funds, stocks, bonds, a dozen or so small businesses, and so many other dealings that we have a storage room dedicated solely to their filing cabinets and a secretary who does nothing but keep everything about them up-to-date, in the computers as well as the paper files. I meant it when I said they were important to the firm, Louie."

"Yet you couldn't do Jimmy's defense?"

"It's not our area, you know that. We're good at what we do, Louie, the best, as far as I'm concerned. I see the other firms, the business lawyers in this town, and we have the upper hand, the experience and the bulldogs to get business and keep it. We really help our clients, and together we all make money. But we'd be lost in the criminal courts, at least for anything as heavy as what Jimmy faced. I asked you because I thought you could do it, and because you're an old friend, Louie. Your name is always on my list of possible referrals, for certain kinds of cases. And it wouldn't have been square to represent Jimmy; there were other issues at stake."

A knock on the door stopped him. He said, "Yes?" A young woman walked in with a sheet of paper. Padgett read it quickly and told the woman, "I'll be right with him. Just another minute." He was running out of time for this old friend. I decided to help him out.

"Let me take a wild shot here, Dave. Jimmy and Lisa Esch haven't always—how shall I say it?—lived up to their parents' ideals. I imagine that the way the Eschs have structured their wealth and the future of their children involves creative incentives for the kids to act right. There are probably conditions on the transfer of the funds from the trustees to the beneficiaries, Jimmy and Lisa. Certain amounts filter down to the kids if certain milestones are reached, maybe when they made it to twenty-one. Then other amounts end up in the kids' bank accounts if they accomplish certain goals—things like finishing school, marrying the right person, kicking those nasty drug habits, staying out of prison. The typical aspirations near and dear to proud parents. And because you all set up the trusts, your hands as lawyers would be tied and probably slapped rather harshly if you defended one of the kids in court on something that had the potential to cost the client a fortune if you lost. But, you still administer the trusts, and the firm still makes money in any event, no matter how the criminal charge turns out."

"I can't confirm anything about the Eschs' private financial dealings, and you no doubt can figure that the details are buried so deep that you'd have to be a government bank auditor with years to spare even to get a peek at the records."

He looked at me over the rim of his coffee cup in a way that had to signify I was right but that he'd never admit it.

"But I did tell you, Louie, that the firm had a conflict of

interest. Or at least there could have been a conflict, and we didn't want to be in that position. It was a business decision that should have benefited everyone involved. And that's the way it was going! Jimmy's codefendants were farmed out to the public defender and another court-appointed lawyer, and you did a great job with Jimmy's defense. The only downside has been the garbage dumped on you, and for that, I truly am sorry."

I refused a second shot of cognac, but I let him know that, emotionally at least, he had made me feel a bit better. I shook his hand and showed myself out. Some of my hunches were right. *Pero*—it's the way I am—*me pasó algo.* An itch, no bigger than a pinprick, squirmed among the folds and recesses of my queasy stomach. As I waited for the elevator, I silently added to Padgett's list of "downsides": Jimmy's insides flowing onto his greasy, foul kitchen floor, and Lisa's untimely disappearing act. Dave must not have thought those were business considerations worth noting.

By the time I closed my office door on the foot of a radio newscaster who had nested in my waiting room, I had accepted several essentials. Priscilla ignored me as I made my end run around the newshound, and it was obvious that I had to talk with her, get her back on the bus cruising down Montez Boulevard, not quite yet a superhighway. Case files, legal pads, and telephone messages surrounded me at my desk. Several hours of work waited. The wheels of justice may grind slowly, but they sure don't stop because one of the rusty cogs is in quicksand up to his ears, he can't touch bottom, and a hundred-pound sack of *caca* just landed on his shoulders. Somewhere there had to be a place where I could relax.

I recognized my obligations to Dad and the family, and I had to clear up the Esch stuff one way or another. And Evangelina's wisp clung to the dark side of my brain, something that quivered in pain when I permitted light to penetrate.

But it was essential that I maintain my practice. I needed to see clients, make it to all my courtroom appearances, finish deals and initiate new ones, and counteract the negative stories and headlines that would appear with regularity in the daily papers. If I didn't, then the corner of the world that I had cordoned off for myself would be gone, and Chuey would be proven right—I just didn't have it.

I needed it for more personal reasons, too. The years of sacrifice to finish my education, the decades of patching a business together out of whatever I could hustle, and the countless days and nights of agonizing over my clients and their problems—all would be wasted unless I pulled it together. I had seen too many lawyers come and go, some yanked off the stage by the disciplinary committee of the state supreme court, others casualties of the bottom line— and so many of them had multicultural last names too difficult for court reporters that if I were a more paranoid person, I might suspect a conspiracy of some sort.

I was better than that. It was time to suck it up, *ese.*

7

◆

Hours later, after ten that night, I crawled out of my office, weary but satisfied. I had accomplished minor miracles. Motions in cases that had seemed vague and obtuse only days before had opened up for me into clear and reasonable expressions of legal brilliance. Letters to opposing counsel that I had stumbled over because I had felt jittery about my clients' positions flowed into my minidictaphone, ready for Priscilla's word processor. My last bit of business had been a note on how to approach the Borregos on behalf of the Alvarado sisters.

As a young attorney with the Legal Aid Society, then for a handful of years on my own, I had enjoyed the feeling when I climbed over the top, when I clipped out my work, moved cases and projects forward, and actually practiced law. The points at which I reached those levels of satisfaction had become finer and finer over the years. I blamed any number of things, among them the toll from working against underhanded attorneys, always sensing that my back was against the wall because I wasn't a member in good standing of the club—hell, I didn't even know where the clubhouse was—

and, yes, of feeling a bit burned out because of my clients. But when I reached one of those exquisite fine points, I knew that whether the boys at the bar association cocktail parties wanted me or not, I was a lawyer, and I would always be a lawyer, and there wasn't anything they could do to take that away—well, unless I was convicted of bribery, kidnapping, and murder.

The physical fruit of my labor included a pair of raw eyes and a stiff back. I had hunched over my work as if I were an old jeweler manipulating the miniature innards of an antique watch. I stretched my spine and created bothersome cracks and pops. My body was *chicharrón*. I needed to work out more. How about I needed to work out?

At the door to my building, I breathed in the crisp, cool air. The day had slipped by me and I had missed the warming—the melting and the sunshine that had zapped the remaining snow and black ice. There was a damn good chance that the next morning would be bright and clean and I would be groggy and in a haze, although satisfied that I had made a large-enough dent on the accumulated pile of cases and clients so that I could focus on my own legal problems.

I had checked with the hospital on Dad—no change. I spoke with Graciela, who first jumped on my butt about arguing again with Chuey and then about not being at the hospital with everybody else. She vented, then apologized. I promised to see everyone later, then hung up. I didn't make it to the hospital.

I had ignored calls from reporters and the colleagues who only wanted the latest dirt on good old Louie. I did return a call from Tenorio, but he was out and hadn't dropped by with yet more good news. He still didn't have enough to round me up, no matter how crazily Mrs. Esch performed for Wanda Higgins.

Alton Enoch had called while I was ruining my stomach lining at David Padgett's office. His message simply said that he would try again. No number, no time for the return call.

El que nada debe nada teme. He whose hands are clean has nothing to fear.

I knew I was innocent, at least of the Jimmy Esch killing, but that didn't make me feel secure. The fact that weird, stupid things happen certainly wasn't a new insight. Over the years, I had actually defended some people who were innocent, but that hadn't made the cases any easier. To the contrary, I had to bust my briefcase to keep them out of the joint. The cops and DA were convinced they had closed the net on the right slimeballs, and when I showed the jurors that it just wasn't so, I never was thanked by the prosecutors for ensuring that justice was carried out, that the system was made to work because I had done my job. And sometimes the acquitted didn't finish paying his bill. That reminded me that I owed Ybarra another check before the week was out.

I decided to follow up on the ideas I had played with the night before, when I was still thinking that the whole mess might blow over. First on my list were Mr. and Mrs. Esch. The timing wasn't quite right, but I didn't expect Beatrice and Greg to open their doors to me, so anytime would do.

The streets in Cherry Hills Village were clean—no ice or mud in this neighborhood. I parked a short distance from the Esch house, next to a well-manicured greenbelt that in the day must have been busy with bicyclists, joggers, and pedigreed dogs. I sat in darkness, watching the lights in the house, the silent front door, and a prancing Doberman sniffing the corners of the fenced yard. I thought that seeing the place where Lisa had played as a child might trigger something in my head, give me a flash of insight that would lead me to her, and save my neck, as well. But I saw only a huge impersonal monument that didn't fit with Lisa's sexy smile and bubbling personality. I couldn't picture her on that football field of a lawn, running with her brother into the arms of her doting father—but then, I simply couldn't picture Lisa as a child.

I played these mind games for almost an hour, with a dozen variations. I imagined Jimmy as a rebellious teenager, turning on his friends by sharing top-grade marijuana under the towering blue spruce that provided shade for the back side of the house. Or I envisioned the lavish parties Beatrice Esch had organized for her daughter's birthdays. Lisa had described these parties in horrid detail the night we had been together when, briefly, she fell into a reminiscent mood.

"They were grotesque," she had said. "Always a theme, but nothing as simple as clowns or dinosaurs. Christ, no. My parties were opportunities for my mother to parade me and Jimmy in front of all the neighbors, who never accepted my mother on any kind of equal footing—at least that was what Beatrice thought. These parties embarrassed me, and I'm sure they did just the opposite of what she thought they would do. But how would you react to a party for a ten-year-old spoiled brat that had camels and llamas chewing up the hedges, and a ballerina under a tent, dancing the same routine over and over and over? And ugly and strange foods from countries I had never heard of, and four different bands around the yard and in the house, including a strolling group of mariachis?"

I told her that I thought the mariachis were a nice touch, but she didn't laugh, or smile, or even respond. She hadn't reached that point yet. I didn't ask what the theme of that particular party had been, even though I was very curious.

My reverie was interrupted by the sound of a well-tuned engine quickly accelerating. A silver BMW backed out of the driveway and turned the corner at the end of the block. I had almost let my quarry drive away without picking her up. Mrs. Esch's face was lit up for an instant by the orange glare from a halogen lamp along the bike path. It was easy to see from what side of the family Lisa had inherited her all-American good looks.

I kept her taillights in view, hoping that she hadn't noticed me. I didn't want to think about what would happen if she had seen me and called the cops and was setting me up for an harassment charge, or if she was on her way to the TV station with the latest report on my dubious methods of representing her son.

She hurriedly made it to Hampden, then the freeway entrance. I followed the BMW on I-25 back to the city, and her exit. We drove through the melancholy midnight twinkle of Colorado Boulevard, past Glendale, City Park, and the Museum of Natural History, and then into a neighborhood where the Beamers were owned by drug dealers and gang leaders—a place that should have been unfamiliar to a high-strung, rich white woman with a grudge against her son's lawyer. I followed Mrs. Esch into Alton Enoch's turf.

The lights were on in the house—it seemed the lights were always on at the Enoch household. Mrs. Esch's hurried footsteps mirrored Lisa's energy. She ran to Alton's house, knocked, and waited. The doorway briefly framed Alton's hulk; then he moved back and Mrs. Esch followed. I waited maybe thirty minutes, without any expectation of an explanation from Mrs. Esch or Alton. It wasn't going to happen that night. The temperature had dipped again, and finally the cold got the better of me and I left. I didn't debate reminding Alton that he had promised to call me again.

Chuey and Michael left early the next morning for the hospital, but not before Chuey made it clear that the family expected to see me later. I promised to come by as soon as I finished my "business," which meant meeting with Ricardo to talk over the week's events.

I had reached him by phone, and breakfast sounded like

a good idea. I gave him a brief summary of the previous night's caper. He reminded me that my payment was due. Neither one of us wanted to sit in an office, and the restaurant at I-70 and Federal was a mutual favorite.

Ricardo looked good. I knew I didn't. He sported jogging pants, a bright, colorful Cinco de Mayo sweatshirt, and a baseball cap welcoming the Colorado Rockies. His clean-shaven face practically glowed with vitality. I had shown up in faded, scruffy jeans and an olive-gray turtleneck one size too small. At least my mustache was trimmed.

Huevos à la mexicana did miracles for my brain waves, and I was thinking again, but my standard morning order at Las Palmas couldn't do anything, and never had, for the bags and wrinkles. Ricardo had the chorizo, and for several minutes neither one of us said anything. Saturday mornings are supposed to be like this, I thought—delicious food, strong coffee, a beer or two, Los Bukis on the CD jukebox, and my lawyer building up his confidence to give me yet more bad news.

We sat in a green vinyl booth. Sombreros and serapes draped walls that also supported plastic flowers, plaster parrots, and surreal photographs of beaches and what I finally concluded were motel bedrooms. Shouts and whistles from the kitchen filled the dining room. Buxom waitresses in short skirts hurried by our table but took the time to ask in Spanish if we needed anything else. Long live the Northside!

When at last I had to stop and give my *enchila'o* mouth a break, I said, "Beatrice Esch and Alton Enoch are not my choice for twosome of the year. It makes no sense to me."

Ricardo held a piece of tortilla wrapped around a healthy chunk of his spicy eggs. The food stayed at mouth level, under the shadow of his nose.

"Yeah, it's kinky, I'll give you that. But she could be

there for something totally innocent—at least innocent for those kinds of people."

"Try me."

"She's a grieving mother. She wants to find out more about her son's last days, get the details from the people he knew, his friends. Or maybe Enoch had something belonging to Jimmy and he turned it over to Mrs. Esch. Or anything like that, Louie. Completely innocuous."

"At midnight? I don't think so, Ricardo. Those things are done in the day, probably by one of her errand boys, somebody like Dave Padgett. That visit at midnight wasn't as clean as you want me to think it was."

He twisted his lips into a "well, maybe" grimace. He finished his interrupted move to his mouth and breakfast was over.

Ricardo made a show of paying the bill. He refused my offer of a five for my eggs, then flirted with the giggly Mexican twenty-something who punched in our meal tab on the restaurant's obsolete calculator.

"I'll put it on your statement, man."

Heh-heh. Sure. Since he was in such a generous mood, I asked a legal question.

"You know anything about estates, beneficiaries, challenges to trusts?"

He looked at me as though I had insulted his mother.

"God, man. I haven't even thought about that stuff since law school. If it doesn't happen in a courtroom, I know nothing, Louie. This got anything to do with Esch?"

"Just curious, Ricardo. For future reference."

He thought I was playing around, and he wanted no part of it.

"Louie, you've got to be careful. Spying on Mrs. Esch was dumb. The cops are watching you. Ug was probably sitting down the street from Enoch's house, waiting for you to do something he could knock you on your ass about. Let me handle this case, and you get back to your practice. Leave the private-eye stuff to the paperbacks."

I felt appropriately chastised. Ricardo was supposed to give me counsel and advice—I was paying good money for it. But nobody paid me to accept it.

Ybarra passed on one more piece of information.

"And speaking of doing dumb things. I was at a meeting last night, Louie—the public policy committee of the Hispanic Bar Association. You know those guys. Your TV headlines were the favorite topic of the night. Better than commercials. But I did hear something you might find interesting. One of your favorite cops, Ben Martinez, quit the force. He's leaving town. Very sudden, very unexpected. Gave up a pension, vacation leave, you name it. Got into hot water, too. Something about not enough notice, violating the bargaining agreement. Announced he was on his way to California to work with his brother's security agency— investigations, process serving, rent-a-cops. Some people thought he had it made here in Denver. Wonder why he would do that?"

Martinez's retirement came one day too late, as far as I was concerned. Ricardo left me standing near my car.

"Thanks for the payment, Louie."

I finished the day with Jesús. Brothers, sisters, nephews, and nieces drifted in and out of the room. We didn't talk except for halfhearted attempts at civility. After three days on watch, they were haggard and edgy. Still, we were more cordial than usual because we were all scared to hell that Dad was leaving us, and we didn't want to taint any memories we might be making.

For a few minutes, I was alone with Dad. The curtains were drawn and the room was dark except for the chair where I slouched, which was near a night-light that one of my sisters had brought to his room. He mumbled in Spanish through dreams whose imagery I could never imagine. He tossed and turned in his bed, threatening his tubes and wires, and more than once I jumped to his side to help him. Finally, Jesús's face relaxed, and I convinced myself that he was napping, half-awake, half-asleep, one of his favorite tricks, especially when I dropped by for a visit and my griping about lawyer stuff bored him.

I talked, more to myself than to Dad.

"Why is this happening to me? What did I ever do to any of these people to deserve this? Why would Mrs. Esch visit a thug like Enoch? What do you say, Dad?"

He moved his lips to make room for more mumbles and incoherent noises. He looked like a baby talking in his sleep. I sat and watched, listening and thinking about what Dad might have said.

Dr. Webster had told Graciela that Jesús had fluid in the lungs, the beginnings of pneumonia, an irregular heartbeat, and was suffering from general exhaustion. They were watching his blood pressure, his breathing, and other vital signs that could signal a significant breakdown of his body systems. For a man who had to be at least seventy, any one of his problems could be critical. That's the way she explained it, and I didn't want to talk it over with Webster. Whatever he said couldn't help.

Even Chuey was tense.

The day was a grim, stiff movie of hospital food, walks around the block for air, and relatives either too congenial or quiet—a day without an in-between mood, and without any good feeling about what would happen to Dad. We were all strung out because of the waiting, and we saw no end. By the time I left the hospital, I had developed a headache that stretched from the center of my skull to the base of my spine. Chuey and Michael disappeared, and I forced myself to focus on the Esch mess.

Again, it was too late to visit Mrs. Esch. Ricardo had been right—the cops certainly were watching her place. At the minimum, a patrol car would be driving by periodically. I played with confronting Alton Enoch. I quickly quit playing. If Alton talked to me, it would be when he wanted, when he was ready. Except for the first message, I hadn't heard from him since my casual drop-by.

Glory Jane Jacquez intrigued me. She had been charged along with the boys, and now her case would enjoy the overflow from whatever happened with Jimmy's and Alton's cases. Ms. Jacquez had witnessed the details of the night of the arrest. She knew Jimmy and Alton, apparently quite well. Someone in Denver had to understand the connection between Jimmy's killing, Strayhorn's untimely accident, and my smeared reputation—Glory Jane might be that person, maybe unwittingly.

She was a classic, a cutie who courted disaster just by walking in a room. I knew she was a homegirl who had marched through the different divisions of juvenile court behind a parade of delinquency petitions, custody motions, D & N summonses, and a paternity action or two. That was years ago, and now that she was a big girl, her drug bust with Jimmy and Alton could have been just a preliminary to the main event. But Strayhorn was dead, Martinez had booked, the evidence had been suppressed, and the DA's case was deader than my sex life. Everything I knew about Glory Jane, and people like Glory Jane, told me that she had to be celebrating the fortuitous turn of events, and she might be in a talkative mood. All I had to do was stumble across the party.

8

It wasn't as if I had never been through this scenario. Where could I find a friendly Chicana on a Saturday night? The times I had come up with the right answer were distant Toltec history, parables found on codices from a different age. Those times had been important, maybe critical, but I never thought of myself as desperate. Finding Glory Jane was my Saturday-night obsession and there was a desperate rush to my acts. And sex had nothing to do with it.

I showered, changed clothes, had a shot of bourbon and a couple of slugs out of a beer.

El Chapultepec had achieved a fame in the city that other, more expensive bars envied like the rich brat envies the poor boy's way with girls. The jazz dive off Larimer's skid row sat conspicuously close to the location for the under construction baseball stadium, and only a beer bottle's throw away from the recently gentrified lower downtown, "LoDo." The new and still-in-the-planning-stage art galleries, sport bars, restaurants, and parking lots wanted the Pec's customers, but they didn't necessarily want the Pec. My trek began in the bar I used to find myself in every Friday night. That was another story, another time.

The front door was closed to the January night air. Tourists, college students, and two or three jazz fans sweated together, in one another's faces, their bodies grinding slowly in the packed club. I recognized a few old acquaintances, and a group of lawyers from the attorney general's office. There were always lawyers.

The Pec's hot-spot status didn't come from the crowd. The faces changed every night, and they all had different reasons for standing in front of the band, holding up beers and an occasional burrito. The only explanation for me was that the live music was the best in town.

I didn't expect to find Glory Jane, but the Pec was a place to ask questions and leave her name. It was a place that people found during the night, for a song or two, maybe one set, before they passed on to other bars, clubs, and parties. I counted on a simple system of good-time small talk and alcohol-influenced rumormongering. The crowd moved on, and new faces moved in to sweat and drink and cheer for the band, and some of them took my name and Glory Jane's and linked us together.

Nick, behind the bar, and Molly, who filled my orders for beers, promised to keep their eyes open for her, and they would tell others. Frankie, the sax player, a guy I had represented during a brief period of domestic turmoil, nodded and grinned and wondered why I would be asking about Glory Jane.

"Don't get me wrong, Louie. Nothing against Glory J. Shit, man, she's an old friend, a real *old* friend," he emphasized. "I just didn't think you had much in common with her."

"It's business, Frankie. I'm checking on some details for one of my clients, she could be a witness, and, you know, she's been hell to find. Hope you can help out."

"If I see her, I'll tell her, man."

I counted on them, and I expected that sometime during the night, in another bar, somebody would tug at my ear and ask, "Louie, what you need from Glory Jane, that crazy chick?" And he would know where to find her.

I mixed it up. My single-minded search for Glory Jane gave me an excuse to walk the several blocks around the Pec. She could be anywhere, and I could go anywhere, have a drink, mention her name, and check out the next place. It sounded like a plan.

The new bars along Blake and Market were set up perfectly for the Rockies fans that in another three years would inundate the area. I would be one of the thousands who would come for at least one game in every home stand. I counted on my low lottery number for good season tickets, unless Ybarra ate into too much of my Rockies savings account. I was a Rockies fan before the team had uniforms. I anticipated my new life centered on the box scores and standings. Sure, the team would be awful for a few years, but it was baseball, and that was enough, wasn't it? Whatever bad-mouthing I did about the changes to Denver caused by the national pastime included something for myself for being a part of it.

The new stadium had to affect the neighborhood, and that night it was easy to see which way the wind was blowing. Small cultlike art galleries, huddled next to one another in adjoining rooms, had replaced used-furniture stores; sterile pool parlors had risen from the ashes of dilapidated warehouses; and eager, almost embarrassingly polite brewery bars stood where Kerouac and his friends once got stinking drunk, threw up in the gutter, and moved on down the road to write about it.

¡Ay, LoDo! ¡Me dió DoLor!

It took a while, but I did what damage I could to the new beers in the new places, sampled wine at a buzzing opening at one of the galleries, and played a profitable round of pool on the second level of a combination sports bar and buffalo steak restaurant.

At each stop, Glory Jane's name rolled off my lips. I mentioned her, although it was obvious it would do no good. My curiosity about Ms. Jacquez turned into an annoying habit, an idiosyncracy that the law students and computer programmers could later play up for their girlfriends.

"You should've seen this one guy. A drunk Mexican, insisted on playing pool, betting outrageous money. He was sloshed, kept asking about his old lady, Glory Hole something. We just laughed."

And lost the bets.

Guys munching on supernachos or standing next to me in urinals shook their heads. They didn't know me, so how would they know Glory Jane?

I weaved northward, closer to the Pec, near where I had launched my search.

There were still a few blocks on Larimer that hadn't yet lost touch with their roots. Johnnie's Market proudly displayed the goat heads, cow brains, and tripe that any Mexican mama could turn into Sunday-afternoon delicacies. The Mexico City Café sold the greasiest, tastiest taco in Denver.

And Sin Fronteras served anyone who could walk in the door, or get dragged through it, as long as you looked and acted like you meant it. I ambled through the heavy metal door and into the smoke, noise, and tension of the bar, where I probably was the only one who was legal, and yet I was the one the cops most likely would arrest, at least that night.

This was a Spanish-only place, and it definitely would be gone when the new stadium opened and the city big shots prostituted the new image for all the media hype one little city stuck between Kansas City and San Francisco could muster.

The air was thick and stuffy with the smells of working-men. Laborers from the packinghouse, 'cheros who sweated in the kitchens of the best restaurants, dog-food renderers, and drug dealers on a break from their curbside capitalism jostled for space at the cracked bar. Groups of men in cowboy hats and western shirts draped around wobbly tables, laughing loudly, cussing, slapping arms and backs. Couples lewdly bounced across a corner that served as the dance floor. Music filled the room, from somewhere.

I realized one good thing. There were no lawyers in this joint, except for me, and I was so far into the beer and the shots of tequila I had foolishly shared with the AG's boys back at the Pec that I felt invincible, and secure in my secret identity as Little Louie Montez, Northsider.

The snappy yet sad music forced me to shake my butt. The words to the songs mirrored the experiences of the men who remembered home and families thousands of miles away, or lost girlfriends who lived around the corner. The sadness mixed with the booze, and I was a goner—just another weepy Mexican, regretting choices and missed chances. Drinking, broken hearts, sudden death from a card game—*sentimiento, sufriendo penas, y la mujer ingrata*—what could I do when that kind of emotion was carelessly spewed all over me, the guy whose angel had dumped him, the guy whose father was deathly ill, the guy who—

The jab on my shoulder was supposed to have been a tap to get my attention. The slurred female voice said, "Hey, lawyer. What the fuck Glory Jane Jacquez mean to you?"

I had reached the stage where talking to myself didn't seem odd. I mumbled, "Some nights, it's like that."

The voice screeched in my ear.

"I said, what business you got with Glory Jane?"

I turned to the voice and stared into a pair of hard-core eyes that reflected visions of pain and beauty, something I never understood.

It was Glory Jane, of course. She stood very close, bending and weaving from the crush of the customers and the effects of the Sin Fron's ghastly version of margaritas. Her breasts squirmed beneath her loose blouse, straining to pop out in freedom, and I was tempted to hold them to secure their modesty. The point of Glory Jane's knife, pressed against my kidney, brought me back to the immediate agenda.

"Glory Jane, it's me, Louie Montez. I represented Jimmy Esch. We talked once about the case, at Jimmy's place. I have to ask you a few questions."

"Hell, man. You're crazy! You know what happened to Jimmy. Talking about him is the last damn thing I'm gonna do, especially to you. They say you had something to do with Jimmy's murder. I ought to even the score for him. . . ."

She twisted the blade and I felt the point puncture my skin. I grabbed her wrist and thumb and tried to separate one from the other. She screeched and jerked, called me a motherfucker, and kicked my shin. I expanded the distance between her thumb and the rest of her fingers and the blade fell. It was a small knife, called a jackknife by the Boy Scouts, and it must have cost her fifty cents at the flea market. I was a bit embarrassed by my reaction to such a trivial weapon.

I hugged her as fiercely as I could and pointed her toward the door. To anyone else in the bar, we were just another Saturday-night prelim. I led the squirming Glory Jane out of the bar. I looked back and saw a dark hand pick up the knife, but there were too many people to match a face with the hand.

She continued to cuss and wrestle. I dragged her away from Sin Fron and the curious gawks of the arriving customers. Finally, we tumbled at the corner, where we rolled around on the sidewalk until she finally quit, exhausted and too drunk to finish the fight. We were streaked with mud and grime.

"You asshole. Now what? You made me forget my coat. I'm gonna freeze my *nalgas*. You fucking pig, you'll pay for my blouse."

One of the anxious breasts had made good on its earlier threats, and it now sat exposed through a tear in the shiny material that earlier in the evening must have looked good on Glory Jane. She made no move to cover herself. She lay on the sidewalk and I sat next to her, trying to remember why I had wanted to talk to her in the first place.

My shirt was also ripped, where the blade had made its entry, and a thin line of blood creased my side.

"Christ, Glory Jane. I didn't want to hurt you. But that may change if I don't quit bleeding."

She craned her neck to see what I was talking about. The freed breast flopped around with her movement and I quietly marveled at the darkness of the aureole and the sturdiness of the nipple.

Then she erupted in laughter. I shook my head, thinking that she was too far gone to do me any good. She lay on the sidewalk, her body shaking with laughter, and that made me smile, then laugh, and in a minute I lay next to her on the cold street, laughing.

"Glory Jane, please. We need to talk, about Esch and Alton and what the hell is going on since you guys were arrested. You need to help me, and I'll help you, whatever I can do, whatever that is."

"Hell, Montez, you can't do anything for me. Jimmy bought it, and Strayhorn, too. One day, it'll be me. One way or the other. Only Alton walks, the man no one can touch."

I couldn't tell if she meant something specific or if she was speaking generically, waxing philosophical about the fleeting nature of existence. I sat up, and she joined me. We shook the dirt out of our hair and brushed the remnants of the storm off each other's backs.

"Don't you know how stupid it is to ask around for somebody, acting like a cop, when you ain't a cop? Especially when people are getting bumped off. I'm psycho enough without you making life even tougher. Damn, Montez."

"I found you, right? And now we can talk."

"And what you want to know, man? You know all about my run-ins with the law. Every fucker in this town seems to know all about how they took my girls from me when I was fifteen, and how I did a stretch of time before I was twenty."

Yeah, I knew that.

"But tell me, Montez. You know that I graduated from community college over a year ago? You know that I got a job with a bunch of do-gooders counseling unwed mothers from the projects? You know that I ain't been busted—hell, I ain't even been in trouble—for years and years. I'm almost thirty, Montez, and I'm clean."

That was hard to believe, considering how she had introduced herself to me earlier.

"Then what was this all about? I just wanted to talk."

"These are bad times for me. I'm trying to tell you. You scared the shit out of me tonight. Everywhere I went, somebody said there was a guy asking about me, somebody I didn't think I knew. Jimmy getting killed and all. And I likely got a little loaded. I still party, man. I didn't say I turned into a saint. Come on, let's get a drink."

"What?"

"Of coffee, Montez. A drink of coffee."

We patched ourselves together, including returning the wayward breast to its proper place. I helped as much as I could. The drunken men leaving Sin Fron were louder than before, and more curious. They made me uncomfortable and the way Glory Jane reacted it was easy to see that she didn't feel right about the crowd, either.

She said, "Let's go to the pawnshop. Clyde's always there, especially on Saturday night. He'll have coffee. He's an old friend. We can talk there, away from everybody."

"At a pawn shop? Why not a coffee shop?"

"On this block? Get real, Louie."

At the corner, she stopped for a breather. I took advantage of the time to talk.

I asked, "How long you known Esch and Enoch?"

"Too long, man, too long. Those guys are part of my old crowd, guys that stick like dog shit on cheap shoes. The Eschs have been nothing but bad news. I just couldn't shake them."

"They almost cost you a stretch, on a petty dope stop."

Her head rocked up and down, side to side, and her hands twitched in circles above her head.

"Yeah, man! I know, I know! Talk about stupid! When Martinez and Strayhorn busted us, it was the same as always. Too much dope and not enough brains to do it right. Enoch and Esch didn't like each other, but they always ended up with each other. From one setup to another—poor rich Jimmy Esch, tagging along after big bad Alton Enoch. Mutt and Jeff. Made me laugh, man. A real toot."

I followed her weaving ass to the Coral Pawn and Loan Shop around the corner from Sin Fronteras, next to a deserted warehouse, gloomy and treacherous-looking. The doors and windows to the pawnshop were covered with bars, wire, and alarm tape, and I couldn't see any light. But Glory Jane avoided the front and eased along the side of the building, next to the warehouse, into a dead-end alley littered with wine and malt-liquor bottles, paper bags, empty glue tubes, and discarded pieces of clothing.

"What are you doing, Glory Jane? Where—"

"Clyde crashes back here sometimes, above his store, really. But you can get in only through his side door. I'll knock and he'll let us in and then—"

The sound came from behind us, in the darkness. We were hedged in between the pawnshop and the warehouse, and I couldn't see anything in front of me except Glory Jane's shadow. A kicked bottle slid across the alley.

I whispered to her back, "Duck behind the bin and stay down. I'll try to see who the hell it is."

She reached back and grabbed my wrist. Her hand was hot and sweaty. She held me for an instant, then disappeared behind a trash Dumpster propped against the warehouse. She didn't say good-bye. She said, "I knew this wasn't any good. That fucking Esch."

I stretched against the brick wall and sucked in my stomach. The laughter, music, and shouts from the bar echoed in the cramped space Glory Jane had led me to, and I wondered if she had set me up. Her breathing was loud, but it sounded hollow and useless.

And there was something else, too. A shape floated in and out of my vision, and I felt the presence of another person. I couldn't see anything for sure, but he was there, only a few feet from me. He inched forward, and he was going to hit me with whatever he held. I swung my fist at what I thought was his chin. My hand glanced off his face. He said something I didn't recognize and stumbled backward.

I jumped for him, but in the darkness I didn't see the bottle. My feet rolled out from under me and I thudded against the brick wall. The breath was knocked from my lungs and I had to lean against the wall. The shape grabbed my shoulders and spun me around. Something hard and heavy smashed my nose and I fell to the ground. I was on all fours when a foot crashed into my back and sent me sprawling. I was out of breath, bleeding heavily from my nose.

Another hit was coming. I rolled across the space, hoping to escape any more punishment. Scuffling and wrestling sounds came from behind me. The scream pierced the night, and the noises from the bar stopped. Someone ran; then I was flattened again with another kick to my back. I fell, wedged against the building, staring up into the night sky, ready to pass out from the pain along my spine, choking on my blood. A minisun exploded over me, casting the alley in a ghostly grayish light.

"Who is that? What's going on out here?"

A grizzled elderly man in a grimy beret broke the glare of the dim lightbulb. He stood a foot or two above the alley, framed by a doorway.

I made a quick assumption and croaked out pathetic words. "Clyde, help. Glory Jane . . ."

He fixed his stare at me, his eyes rolled in surprise and terror, and then he jumped from his door to the alley. He tried to keep both me and the bin in his line of vision. He moved slowly, very slowly, as though he didn't really want to get to where he was going. He stopped when he got to Glory Jane. Her little knife had ripped out most of her throat, and now it was lodged in her eyeball. Blood covered the patched blouse and most of the area around her body. Clyde forced himself to look away from Glory Jane and down at me. The gun in his hand shook with fear and anger. He leveled it at my head, and I hoped nothing would happen until the cops ran into his alley. The music from the bar cranked up again, and a wild drunken woman's laugh echoed across LoDo.

9

---◆---

The arrest, the searches of my house, office, and car, the charges, the hearings, the stories in the papers and on TV, even the suspension of my license by the Colorado Supreme Court—none of it compared to the crap I had to put up with from my older brother in return for his word to take it easy with Dad.

"Ay, Little Louie," he snickered.

He rocked on the balls of his feet. We stood outside Jesús's room. Graciela, Roberta, Juanito, and Michael surrounded us as we hammered out the details of what I hoped was a truce that would include Chuey's cooperation. The family would go along with what we agreed to, and I didn't expect any resistance from anyone except Chuey. Even Graciela could see that Jesús didn't need the hassle of knowing all the details of my crisis.

Chuey's lecture ranged far and wide. He covered every real and imagined offense that I had committed since I was three years old. He worked himself into a lather and launched into his pet accusation—that I had prevented him from finishing school because all the money went for the expenses of my education.

"Your grades made you the best hope for someone to graduate, so Dad forgot about the rest of us and gave everything to you."

I acted as though I was about to set the record straight, but Roberta and Graciela frowned at me and I shut up.

"You're the one we should be able to go to with our problems, with questions, so we can get advice, help. But you're never around, Louie, or you're too busy, or some *mierda* that always pops up when one of us needs you."

He was referring to my reluctance to represent him every time he was dragged to county court by a creditor or cited with a contempt citation by his ex-wife because of his tardy child-support payments. I had taken my share of lumps as Chuey's lawyer and years ago I had drawn the line. My decision had never set right with him.

Eventually, at the urging of the others, Chuey promised to participate in the great cover-up. No one would tell Dad more than he absolutely had to know about my problems until we thought he was well enough to deal with them. We would keep him away from newspapers and news programs that might have something about my case. And we would screen visitors. We didn't want anyone to express casual condolences—"Sorry to hear about Louie"—although I was sure that people told him that all the time anyway.

The monitors of the legal profession didn't waste time. My office was closed down by the state supreme court until the shadows of murder and bribery were chased away or I was permanently locked out of the business. Sure, it was a temporary suspension of my license—after all, I hadn't yet been convicted—but it did the trick. The reason for the suspension was couched in the language of the rules of procedure regarding lawyer discipline. The justices thought they had reasonable cause to believe that I had engaged in conduct that posed an immediate threat to the effective administration of justice.

Call me loco, but I appreciated the irony. *The People of the State of Colorado* v. *James P. Esch* had been one of my most successful cases. My arguments on behalf of Jimmy Esch had resulted in a good decision, and working for him had rejuvenated my jaundiced outlook about the law. How appropriate that Jimmy Esch may have been one of my better-represented clients, since he also apparently was my last client, and the client who brought down the always-shaky Montez house of business cards.

I never did get the chance to follow up on the Alvarado complaints against their neighbors. Priscilla politely excused herself from further involvement with my life, vanishing into the place where secretaries go to become paralegals. My remaining clients demanded their files and my withdrawal from their cases. Law school buddies refused to acknowledge me in the courtrooms as I went through the procedural gyrations necessary to pull the brakes on my law practice.

The rest of it turned into a drawn-out legal affair orchestrated by Ybarra and Dan Galena, the DA assigned to my case. I watched, bored mostly, not excited by the flurry of motions Ricardo drew up, nor by his occasional intermediate victory.

The bribery charges were disposed of rather quickly. There wasn't anyone left alive who had any connection to the fix on Strayhorn, except me, if you believed Wanda Higgins, and I wasn't talking.

As far as the press was concerned, my fate was a done deal. Overnight, I had turned into the "well-known Hispanic attorney" and my life was summed up as "currently facing charges that carry a possible death penalty." When my name appeared, it was usually followed by the phrases "accused of bribery and the murder of James Esch, wealthy scion of Beatrice and Greg Esch," and "a suspect in the unexplained disappearance of the only Esch daughter." The reporters gloated about my past brushes with the disciplinary committee of the bar, my youthful misadventures, and some of my unsavory ex-pals. Once or twice, something about my cases, my career, appeared, but that stuff was not as interesting as the speculation that DA Galena indulged in whenever he had a chance.

"Of course, we haven't found Miss Esch's body, yet, but we are convinced that her abduction resulted in her death and that she may have had information about the bribery scandal that threatened police officers who had dealings and connections with Montez."

Gallina Galena and I were old antagonists. That's one problem with toiling in the trenches of the legal system for more than twenty years. There weren't too many metro-area judges, opposing counsel, and district attorneys I hadn't run into, literally as well as figuratively, and the outcomes hadn't always improved my bleak outlook on the state of legal affairs.

Galena had a well-earned reputation for tough prosecutions. He jumped in each fray with every ounce of pious fervor his tall, lanky body could generate. He spent an inordinate amount of time on jury selection, for a DA, and defense attorneys had to admire his skill at preserving at least one indignant law-and-order type on every jury. Too many of the hired guns had experienced the sinking feeling of having their ace-in-the-hole juror exposed and banished from the courtroom because of the holy wrath of St. Galena.

My defense of a small-time con man named Salvador "Pico" Pinella offered a good example. Pico faced first-degree assault and armed robbery charges. It wasn't Pico's style; he was more the flimflam, sneak-your-money, thank-you-ma'am kind of crook, but, in one case at least, he had been with the wrong people at the wrong time. I thought he should have been offered something by the DA—maybe a lesser degree of assault. But Galena would have none of it.

He went to the mat and Pico and I went with him, although I had to pry Pico from his apartment on the morning of the first day of trial. He was so scared that he was about to run, and he would have if I hadn't arrived and offered him a ride to the courthouse.

Galena and I fought for two days over a jury and I finally had to complain to the judge about what I concluded were his racist tactics to preserve the purity of his jury. Almost every black and Chicano called to the panel had been excused by Galena, or maneuvered into making statements that he used to get a cause ruling from the judge. In chambers, while we sat around the judge's conference table, he explained his tactics more frankly than I had expected.

"Sure, I excused Mr. Gomez. He had long hair and showed up late for court. He could be a social misfit, and he didn't exhibit proper respect for the Court. Mr. Johnson wore a T-shirt—that's not appropriate. And Ms. Gallegos— what do you expect, Your Honor? She's divorced, comes from a small town down south, works as a hotel maid, and quit junior college before she finished her first year. I don't want quitters on my jury."

His righteousness almost silenced me. But I recovered.

"Your Honor! This is exactly what I'm talking about. He's pulling out every stereotype from the Ku Klux Klan handbook! I'm moving for a mistrial!"

Galena stood up and I prepared for a level of argument that usually doesn't happen in a judge's office. Instead of the physical confrontation that I thought he was preparing for, Galena continued with his buttery rationalization for his prejudiced outlook.

"Judge, it's no secret. Prosecutors want older, established, well-educated people who have strong feelings about crime. And I won't be intimidated by Mr. Montez's arguments and objections into keeping prospective jurors I would otherwise excuse if they were white, just because they're minorities."

In the end, though, the judge warned him, he backed down on a couple of jurors of color, and the first trial ended with a hung jury. We worked out a plea bargain after that.

At the close of one of the motions hearings on the Esch case, Galena surrounded himself with reporters and cameras. It was his day for sound bites. Detective Tenorio stood at attention next to the DA, a scowling soldier in the dirty war against crime and corruption, ready to do the unsavory but necessary tasks that Galena required, including bringing down a brother who had gone bad. Ug's sport coat looked like the last piece of a carpet-remnant sale.

"It's cases like these that are really sad—on the one hand, because we're forced to bring the full weight of the criminal justice system against a man who once was trusted and accepted in that system: a lawyer who abused and corrupted his license to practice law. But the other, positive side of cases like this is that I get the opportunity to prove that the law plays no favorites, that even if you are a successful, well-known lawyer, this DA, at least, will do all in his power to bring justice to this case, to bring justice to the tormented and tortured Esch family."

That's the first time I realized I had been successful, forget well known.

We settled in for the long haul on the murder charges. I was accused of killing Jimmy and Glory Jane, apparently because they might have implicated me in the about-to-be-exposed bribery plot that no one could prove. Ricardo wasn't concerned about Jimmy. That was thrown in for padding by the DA, but we all knew that the People of the State of Colorado had nothing but my unfortunate timing, and, so far, that wasn't enough to reserve a seat for me in the Cañon City gas chamber.

Glory Jane, though—she was a problem. Clyde Beech swore that he saw me attack Glory Jane and then trip and fall as I tried to run away. What he saw, of course, was the killer run over me after he finished his business with Glory Jane. But the old guy had his story, and the more often he repeated it for anyone willing to film him in his pawnshop or to take his picture pointing to the spot where he found Glory Jane's body, the more he believed it. There was enough circumstantial evidence in addition to his eyewitness testimony that even Ricardo suffered an attack of fickle nerves.

A dozen patrons of Sin Fronteras remembered me arguing with Glory Jane in the street, recalled seeing me assault and knock her to the ground, then chase after her into the darkness. Eager, believable, and sincere customers of various clubs and art galleries in LoDo selected my picture as the strange drunk guy who had seemed particularly fixated on finding the woman who later turned up dead.

I especially appreciated Alton Enoch's statement that I had pounded on his door, late, waking him up, and that he had had to deal with a half-delirious, out-of-place weirdo who asked strange questions about Glory Jane Jacquez, an old friend of the family. And he went on to say that Jimmy Esch had been a close personal friend, and that Strayhorn hadn't been that bad, either. It turned out I was the only guy in town who wasn't Alton's friend.

I didn't expect to walk. As far as I knew, I hadn't done anything to warrant a traffic ticket, much less the complete breakdown of my life. But that's not the way these things work. I had enough money saved to keep Ricardo on the case—I said good-bye to my Rockies season tickets—and the legal theatrics were under control. The DA was just full enough of himself to make a dumb mistake, and guiltier men than I had floated away on the gossamer wings of such mistakes. That's how this mess had landed on me in the first place.

Jenny Rodriguez, Evie's stepsister and the only ex-client who admitted she knew me, offered support. She was a community activist and she thought her talents could help.

"Louie, let me organize a meeting, see how it goes. We can raise hell about the one-sided publicity about your case, and the special treatment reserved for the Eschs. I've got neighbors whose sons have been shot down in plain view of over a dozen witnesses, months ago, and no one's been arrested. I haven't seen any newspaper headlines screaming out the lurid details of the killers' arrests. The DA hasn't pontificated about 'justice' for the 'tormented and tortured' families of murdered Chicano youth. Your case will help us make an important point."

Although I liked her use of the word *pontificated*, eventually I nixed her plan. Glory Jane had been a Chicana, I reminded Jenny. And I wasn't in the mood to assume the symbolic role of oppressed pigeon.

But I knew. Deep in that corner of my heart that hadn't been scarred by Evangelina, that hadn't dried up from years of playing law-and-order games with people I didn't like, and that still pumped blood oxygenated with the fresh air of reality, I knew.

The jurors would be presented with a short, dark, foreign-looking man who had been given every chance their great country could offer. They would watch a jumpy lawyer defendant who had to have had more breaks than they, given the recent eras of affirmative action and political correctness, and the irrebuttable presumption that all ethnic professionals reaped unfair benefits during those eras. They would naturally take note of the wealthy, matronly, and sophisticated Mrs. Esch and sympathize as she fell apart in her ringside seat, or while Galena delicately guided her through her testimony on the witness stand. He *would* find a way to have her talk to the jury. They would sit entranced as she pointed her diamond-encrusted fingers at the usurper, at the man who didn't belong in the courtroom except where the DA had put him—in the defendant's chair. They would concentrate on the words of DA Galena as he poured out his heart and demanded his justice for the dead and missing Esch children. They would measure the Peop le of the State of Colorado against Luis Montez, they would weigh the evidence, replay the arguments, and remember who they were and whom and what they represented, and, in the end, they would turn their backs on me and send me on my way, never thinking about it again.

Ricardo waltzed around his desk like a dancing bear twirling on broken glass. The DA had offered a deal. What did I want to do? I wasn't listening. We both knew I wouldn't cop to a plea, and he didn't want to recommend it. He had rediscovered his confidence and thought there was a chance. He believed he could punch a hole in reasonable doubt because the DA's case had too much circumstantial evidence, and Clyde and Alton were perfect targets for his cross-examination skills. He was willing to risk it, and I thought that was a grand gesture on his part. But he was a conscientious lawyer. He relayed the offer to me and pressed for an answer.

"So what's the word, Louie? Galena wants your ass, but his boss is queasy about the possible rabble-rousing. He doesn't want to tangle with Jenny Rodriguez's crowd. The line is that you get to avoid the death penalty because you're a lawyer." He paused, took a breath. "You know what I think about it. What do you want to do, Louie?"

My basis for making a decision had gaping holes. I didn't know how well Ricardo would handle Clyde, Alton, and the elusive Mrs. Esch. I didn't know how well I would handle Galena. Consequently, I didn't know whether the offer was good or bad.

But there were several truths I did know.

I remembered Jesús telling me about kites and pants and the devil who cheated at cards. I remembered the way he tumbled his kids across the room, and the smile on my mother's face when he dipped a piece of tortilla in the bean juice bubbling in the black pot on the hot stove. And at that instant, I understood what all that meant.

"There's only one thing I really want to do, Ricardo. One thing."

He looked at me, anticipating an answer, and when I said nothing, he sat down.

"Well, what? What do you want to do, man?"

"I want to hit for the cycle against the Dodgers."

Part II

10

Crouched in his old rocker, covered with a mangy, thin blanket, and without words, Jesús asked questions I wouldn't answer. His bony hands gripped a creased, shredded Mexican paperback. His practice was to hold it in front of his good eye to bring on sleep.

Finally, he said, "*Basta*, Louie. You stay around here all day, feeding me, reading, listening to music, dusting the house. Damn, this house wasn't this clean when your mother was alive! You need to get out, do something."

He wheezed, tried to catch his breath. Although the spring weather had been warmer than I had expected, my father endured chills, all the time insisting that his health was fine.

A weakness from his hospital stay had remained with him, and his days were filled with reading, nodding off, and talking with the family on the phone, or playing poker with my sons. Eric and Bernardo had started visiting again, at least once a week. They practiced the Spanish he had taught them and that now they used so proudly when they were with him.

"Dad, I have to keep a low profile. My case, Ybarra—"

"Don't give me that horse manure. ¿Quién es el estúpido? I didn't say go out and raise hell. A movie? Have a nice dinner someplace. I'm getting tired of your hanging jeta and sad face."

My dad had a way with words.

We had gone through a series of crises and false alarms that had exhausted us. The last days of Jesús's hospital stay had been an out-of-focus counterpoint to my own crisis, a balance of disasters that kept life in perspective. Jesús, at least, had survived. My own fate was less certain.

I hadn't been more than a few blocks from Dad's house since the day the hospital finally released him, almost a week after Glory Jane's killing.

I took over as his nurse. The rest of the family said their good-byes, although at least one of them called each day. Chuey threatened to return, to do the job right, but if it happened, it happened, I reasoned, and I would deal with that when I had to.

I spent hours that easily turned into days with books, music cassettes, and watching Dad and his changes. The house didn't need that much cleaning. My father had always been a fastidious man.

I developed an addiction to the mystery novels of a Mexican crime writer, the few that were translated. I immersed myself in the corruption, grime, and sleaziness of Mexico City, laid out in detail with patience and resignation by the writer, and consistently the almost–good guy figured out the case, even though there was some kind of price to pay.

I tripped on jazz, again, tuning out as I listened to Miles Davis, and scrounged the Northside segundas and used record stores for scratchy Charlie Parker. Jesús ignored the music. He wanted to hear only "Valentín de la Sierra"—his favorite song of all time, he told me. "You should memorize that ballad. It might teach you something."

Right, Dad.

If I did anything outside the house, it was usually without purpose. I toured the Westside on a rusty bike I found in Dad's crowded but neat garage. I took an occasional walk through one of the city's parks, which were coming back to life. I didn't drink, stayed out of bars, avoided my old haunts. There was no sense to what I did, and so it was easy.

I fought against being lost in a warm, almost muggy spring of dreamlike destruction. But I was too divorced from coming to grips with my life, and instead, finally, I surrendered to the beat and circumstances of an across-the-border noir author and to the earthy essential African-American musicians who somehow understood where this unhinged, unkempt Chicano found himself.

Ybarra was doing what he could on my cases. I was prevented from practicing law until the charges were resolved, and I didn't see the need to do anything else. Too many people had died for reasons I didn't know, and I wasn't eager to stir the dust of their bones just to keep busy.

The violence had penetrated me to the hilt. I did not consider myself a violent man. And yet, violence had followed me, rubbed up against me, and destroyed people who wandered into the nightmare of my ambit of opportunity: Jimmy, Strayhorn, Glory Jane, Lisa. What had happened to Lisa? What role had I played in what I knew was her awful, bloody ending? When I thought about it too much, a ball of fear and tension throbbed in my chest, my eyes watered, my breathing was forced, and I would turn my face from my sleeping father and permit the silent notes of Miles Davis to save me.

Jesús lazily drifted into one of his naps. I stood to adjust his blanket when the phone rang, and Dad jumped in his seat. The blanket fell to the floor. I picked it up, smiled at him, and dealt with the phone. His crusty reminded me that it wasn't nice to laugh at the old man.

"Hello."

"Hello, Louie."

Man oh man. Just what I needed, and just what I couldn't handle. Her voice moved the room, twirled my head, and kicked my stomach. I felt queasy, and pissed.

"Don't tell me you're in town."

Not quite what I had practiced all those times I had fantasized about this phone call. I had memorized so many good phrases, cusswords, and romantic poems—where were they when I needed them? Where was my aplomb? What had happened to my caustic assertiveness, so she would never know how fucked up I had been over her?

"No, Louie. I'm in L.A. I'm not going back to Denver."

Why was she calling? Only to pour acid in the hole that once had been my heart, apparently. Time to regroup. I thought, Be cool, man, cool. Don't dwell on the feelings her voice is stirring up. Don't let her get to you. Ignore the rushing blood and tight throat and the catastrophe swilling over your core.

"How is Los Angeles? How are you?"

"Louie, I'm fine. This isn't about me. I heard about all your trouble. You're famous, even out here. The lawyer who killed his client, the cop, the witness, everybody. Jenny keeps me posted—you know how she is about us."

She and her stepsister had been talking about me, long distance. I was encouraged.

Evangelina's voice reached the purpose of her call.

"I called to say I hope you're going to be all right. I mean that, Louie." Before I could stammer a response, she added, "Is there anything I can do?"

I had picked myself off the floor, and thought I could deliver a few thrusts of my sword of retribution. I turned my back to Dad, who clucked his teeth and shook his head.

"Get serious. You run out on me, decide that you can't stick it out, and now you want to help? And what the hell do

98

you think you can do? Type up my will? Son of a bitch, son of a bitch. I don't need all this shit, I don't need—"

She stopped my tantrum by breathing into the phone and whispering one word.

"Luis."

That's all she said, but it was everything I wanted to hear.

"Damn, Evie. I need you, baby. I need you."

"Don't get sidetracked. You're not fighting this, Luis. I know how you are. This is the biggest case you'll ever have, and I've no doubt that you've been moping around your father's house, waiting for them to drag you off to Cañon City. I called your house, and the line's been disconnected. I should've just called Jesús first. I hope he's not letting you get away with your act." She didn't know about Dad's illness. "But I will help. That means I called to tell you to wise up, Louie. Ain't nobody going to do it for you, except you. It's only your life. That's never seemed to mean much to you, but it meant everything to me, once. Pull it together."

Our blowups had often had their roots in Evie's lectures. I wasn't man enough to pay attention when she tried to make me understand, even when she was right. She didn't have the patience to work through my defenses, even when she was wrong. And so we often resolved nothing, and only the smoke of frustration remained of the fire that once had been our love. Hey, I didn't invent the war between the sexes. I just fight it, man.

I backed off. I turned around and Dad scowled at me. He knew Evie was on the line. He liked Evie and couldn't believe she'd let me hang around with her for those few months. I took a deep breath and tried to stay calm.

"Evie. I get it. I have to get off my butt and work to keep it out of prison. You don't think I want to get convicted, do you? It's just that there's not a hell of a lot I can do. Ricardo's pulling out all the stops; he's jamming on my case. But

Galena, you know how he is, and Tenorio's leaning on everybody I know to dig out as much dirt as he can on me. He's a very busy man."

"Yeah, Ug. That's the best and worst thing about your case. I don't understand how you ended up in all this mess, Louie. But from what I've read, and from what people back home have told me, none of this makes sense."

She had talked to people about me. I had been on her mind, and she had asked her old friends about my case, my troubles. I decided that I would take that as a positive sign.

Oblivious to my head trips, she continued her analysis of my case.

"Who bribed Strayhorn? Jimmy Esch had the money but not the brains. And if there wasn't any bribe, then why all the official pressure on Strayhorn? And if Strayhorn's dead, why kill Esch?"

I didn't have to say it. It all made sense only if I was as guilty as Galena and Tenorio had already proven to the press.

"What's your hit on this, Louie? What do you think's going on? Do you and Ricardo have a theory?"

Our only theory was that I didn't do it, and Galena couldn't prove otherwise. Not much, but it was all I had.

"There's a reason, somewhere, Evie. I have to fly a few kites and see what turns up. A little detective work."

"You worry me, Louie. The way you talk, the way you are, *viejo*. Kites and detectives. But if it means you're going to do something, then I guess it's all right."

Oh yeah, it was all right. It was more than all right. She had called me *viejo*, the first time in months. It definitely was all right.

Before I did anything, I ran it down for Jesús. He gave me only a few words, but they were important, for both of us.

"Because you're my son . . . that means more than just

that you once lived in my house. Make this thing right. *Vamos a ver qué va a pasar.* Whatever happens, the family, you, me, your brothers and sisters . . . we will all still be here."

I could only say, "Thanks, Dad."

I had to start with Ben Martinez. The Esch arrest was the beginning, the fulcrum of my agony, and Martinez was there. He was one of only two from that ill-fated group who were still alive, and Alton Enoch wasn't on my short list of engaging conversationalists. Martinez's sudden career change had to be a result of the Esch case—wasn't everything? His need to avoid the truth, and consequences, of his role was transparent, awkward, but it seemed to have worked. He had slipped away to San Diego.

I didn't want to leave town. I was an accused multiple murderer who no longer had certain basic rights, such as the freedom to travel. Judge Ayala had made a point of lecturing me about my responsibilities at the bail hearing, and he had relented only when Ricardo had returned with his own lecture about my years in the legal profession, my good deeds for the community, and my strong ties to the city. Galena had jumped in the fray with a flourish. He demanded a half a million for the security of the public. He let the judge know that "the proof is evident, and the presumption is great," and, as if anyone had forgotten, we were talking about first-degree murder. The judge gave me a slight break and set my bond at $150,000. My father and I hocked everything we owned—houses, office equipment, and savings bonds—so I wouldn't have to mingle with some of my ex-clients in jail. Jesús's worldly accumulations were all at risk.

And, if I had to take off, why not L.A., where I could accidentally run into Evangelina? But it wouldn't work out that way. I had her number and that was it. Would I use it if we ended up in the same state?

My problem was pulling off my vanishing act without screwing up worse than I already had. Running would convince everyone who had any doubts about my guilt—all three of them.

When I thought about it, though, I knew it would be easy. I had been the invisible man for most of my life. After I realized what it meant, it amazed me, and angered me, too, but I had accepted it. I'd enter a room, and no one would say anything to me; no one would catch my eye or engage in the small talk that surrounded me. I hated cocktail parties, receptions, icebreakers—anything that required me to meet new people and actually talk with them, and the main reason was my invisibility.

I sometimes grabbed a person I knew, looked him in the face, and forced an acknowledgment. The lucky target invariably would blink, take a second look, then say, "Hey, Louie, how you doing?—didn't see you."

This happened most often with white people, at bar committee meetings, task forces, even court appearances. The people in the meeting had no idea what I looked like, what my name was. If I saw one later in the street or an elevator, I'd say hello, and the guy would look around, maybe step back, and say hello in return, to be polite, but he wouldn't know me. He answered because I wore a tie and my hair was usually trimmed, and that might mean I was safe. At the next meeting, he would act as though he knew me, but he wouldn't remember me from the elevator. I was a minority filling a slot, and that's all he had to know.

Maybe it was me. Maybe I had to wear louder clothes, or speak louder, or do anything louder.

But if I looked for Martinez, and the killer, I could be as quiet as always, and quieter, and vanish quicker than the final dregs of beer at last call.

Martinez had been listed as a witness by both Galena and Ybarra. He was now associated with Big M Investigations—"We're big enough to cover Southern California, and small enough to fit in a closet." I could have tried calling him on the phone, or waited to ask questions at his eventual deposition by Ybarra. But that wouldn't have been as fun, or productive.

I decided to dust off my lawyering skills. I had been trained to analyze. I knew how to conduct extensive research. I was supposed to know how to employ deductive reasoning. As a lawyer, I was expected to be professional, not emotional; committed to my clients—objective and zealous, in balance.

I had to grasp the facts. From the facts would flow the legal theories and, finally, the conclusions. That's what they told me in law school and that's the way it actually worked out, most of the time.

Ybarra had thick, neatly organized files for my cases. I ensconced myself in his office and pored over the reports, diagrams, memos, letters, and photographs that he had accumulated in my defense. I read the Strayhorn accident reports. I tried to study the Jimmy Esch and Glory Jane Jacquez autopsy reports. In a corner of Ybarra's office, on a small desk he had reserved for me, I waded through arrest and conviction records of everyone in the case, forensic and pathology files on the bodies and crime scenes, inventories of property in the Esch apartment, Lisa's house, Strayhorn's demolished car, and the unfortunate Glory Jane's pockets and wallet. I inundated myself in minutiae, detritus, lists, witness statements, scientific jargon, gruesome eight-by-tens, and junk. It was what any good trial attorney would have to do to prepare, even with the help of a seasoned paralegal. It seemed to be the least that I owed myself.

"Dad's going to need your help. I've got to do some work on the case, help out Ricardo, lawyer stuff. I can't just sit around."

103

Roberta was the smartest kid in the family. She knew I was up to something—she heard it in my voice—and I heard her suspicion in the phone line to Fort Collins.

"If you think so, Louie. It's better if he stays with me, anyway. I'll come down and get him. I'll watch him. Then . . . you'll be at your house?" It was more a suggestion than a question.

"There, and at Ricardo's office. Around, you know. It's bad, *jita.* I'll be very busy. Pick up Dad at my house, not his. He'll be there; that way, you don't have to drive all the way into the Westside."

She held her breath and didn't say anything for several seconds. I tried to speak. "Rober—" She quickly interrupted.

"Be careful, Louie. We all love you. Tell Dad I'll be there in the morning."

The phone clicked into silence, but I held it in my hand and thought about my sisters and brothers, not as adults, but as the children we would always be to one another. Roberta, the little queen, the prettiest, Dad's spoiled one. She lived with her farmer husband and an ever-expanding brood of children. Fertile and pretty, that was Roberta. So much in love with her rugged old man that her affection embarrassed me. Claudio—as Mexican as they come. Ten years older than Roberta. She had found in him the character she couldn't discover in the city boys who paraded to our house all during her high school years.

And now she was my accomplice. I could trust her, and maybe Graciela, although not as quickly. Trust was not a concept I associated with Chuey.

Another chunk of guilt landed on my back.

"Ricardo. Yeah, it's Louie, your favorite client."

I spoke in a rush so he wouldn't have the chance to talk me out of my idea.

"Look, man. Dad's getting to be too much for me, and he's not getting any better. Roberta, my sister, she'll watch him. Been begging me to let Dad move up there, Fort Collins. She's home all day with her kids. Jesús can get twenty-four-hour attention. . . . Yeah, yeah. I know. And, anyway, I've got to work. You're not cheap. I can't afford to just nurse my father all day long. I'm taking a job with Janice Kendall— a paralegal thing. That's all I can do, and Janice, you know her, straight as the crease in your pants. It should make the judge happy. I'll organize files, index depositions, do settings, that kind of crap. It's money I need now. So Dad goes north. Roberta's coming by tomorrow, and I'm going up there to help her out. Easy, *ése*, just for the weekend. I swear, that's it. What am I going to do, run? Where, and with what? Anyway, you're going to get me off, so why should I split, right? Tell Galena—clear it with the court."

He grudgingly approved. I thought of something else.

"Ricardo, can you follow up on one thing? You know Arnold Mansfield, right? You super defense lawyers chum around in the same high altitude. Ask him why he turned down the Esch case. Yeah, that's right."

He didn't understand, but he agreed.

"I'll call, Ricardo, I promise. Yes, *hombre*, I'll check in with the Fort Collins cops. And you, too. I'll call Friday and Saturday and Sunday. Hey, relax. I'll be at work at Janice's office next week. I'm only delivering my dad."

Thursday evening, I made a show of transporting Jesús to my house. I loaded up my old Pontiac with his three suitcases, one overnight case crammed with bottles of medicine, a cardboard box of paperbacks and magazines, and my grouchy father. A group of neighborhood kids volunteered to help. Their version of help meant they crowded around my car and asked Jesús one question after another.

"*Jefito,* where you going now? You just got back from the hospital."

"When we going to play checkers again, Jesús? We ain't played in weeks."

"Don't worry, okay? We'll watch the house, my partners and me. No one will mess with it."

Jesús had me write Roberta's name and phone number on a scrap of paper. He handed it to the boy who had been helping him when he had collapsed.

Dad patiently instructed the kid. "Tony, tell your mother that if anything happens, or she sees something I need to know about, or anything, *tu sabes,* she calls me, collect. I'm counting on you, boy."

The shrimp of a ten-year-old with a *mocoso* nose under a mop of dusty hair carefully filed away Dad's piece of paper in the back pocket of his jeans. His swagger told the others that Dad had cleared the air. It wasn't Tony's fault that Jesús had needed to be rushed to a hospital.

The crowd of boys did one more round of good-byes, then made themselves comfortable on Dad's front porch. We chugged away from the Westside in my smoking, rattling Bonneville. Tenorio had to appreciate how easy it was to tail me.

My story about having Roberta meet Jesús at my house kind of made sense. It had to be screwy enough to set off a buzz in the heads of the cops, but it also had to be so obvious, so out in the open, that they couldn't be too worried about me. They would keep their collective eyes on me all the time I was in Fort Collins, and if I was brash, and stupid, enough to go anywhere except Roberta's farm—zap, the iron teeth of their trap would wrap around my throat and Tenorio happily would jump up and down on them until they were tightly and permanently secured. My short life under the long arm of the law had not improved what Evie had enjoyed referring to as my "cynical imagination."

Chuey had returned late Wednesday. Jesús was surprised to find him waiting for us, but he didn't appear to be bothered by it. And when Roberta showed up at five in the morning, transferred Dad's things to her car, and helped Jesús buckle up in her station wagon, he still didn't say anything about the unannounced visitor. And he only clicked his teeth when Chuey hurriedly climbed into the backseat of the wagon, dressed in one of my "I Don't Speak English Only" sweatshirts, my Rockies baseball cap, and a pair of my sunglasses, and almost immediately began a long nap that must have lasted until they reached Fort Collins.

Ultimately, I didn't trust Chuey, but I was willing to bet that he would do what I asked, if for nothing more than the high he would get by putting one over on the cops, even if it meant he had to pretend to be his *safado* younger brother for a couple of hours.

His response had been succinct when I'd called and approached him about going along for the ride with Roberta and Dad.

"You're a *menso*, Little Louie, a *pendejo*, an idiot, a dope! What you ain't, I guess, is a killer. And Tenorio's a jerk. Yeah, I'll jump in the car for you. I should visit Roberta's family, anyway. And if I borrow a few things from you for the trip, hey, are you my brother or not? Only thing, Louie, and I mean this. I'll break your fucking neck. Don't get Jesús involved any more than he already is. All he needs to know is that I'm going up with them and you're not. What he figures out, he figures out, but at least he's not in it. You've fucked up enough, including Dad's health. Leave it at that."

We both knew that he talked nonsense, and that Dad was in it without us ever having to tell him anything. But if we gave up on our petty fantasies and illusions, then ¿pa' qué vale la vida?

I didn't move from my stuffy bedroom the entire day. I stretched out on the bed, half-sleeping, drifting from Evie to

Lisa to Dad. I crawled to the bathroom, drank water, and crawled back to the bed. I didn't listen to the radio or watch TV. I thought I was becoming invisible.

I had my story in case the cops busted in and found me where they had expected Chuey to be holed up. It had been a simple change in plan, the older brother instead of me; I had too much to do in Denver. It was the same line Chuey would feed the cops if they accosted him on the trip. We still hadn't done anything illegal. If the guys who had been watching my house did see someone moving around in there, it was a good bet that they would assume it was Chuey, maybe looking for something to eat. That would be their assumption, if they made it. I still hadn't done anything illegal.

Finally, a little after one in the morning, when I crept out the back door, moved in the shadows along the fence and into the deserted dark alley—that was when I first admitted that I might have done something illegal.

I scurried through alleys, quiet streets, and along the freeway fence until I boldly strutted into the light and stood next to the highway entrance ramp at Federal. Strapped around my waist was a slim bundle of bills—the remains of my law business, money I originally thought would end up in my lawyer's bank. I wore jeans, my old square-toed boots, a warm flannel shirt, and a jean jacket. I carried a backpack that held a few essentials and a file folder crammed with copies I had made of documents from Ricardo's file. The folder represented my last connection to the legalities of my case.

The overall effect, I hoped, was that of a slightly aged, nonthreatening drifter who could be from Mexico and might be heading for his next job. I thought I looked as inconspicuous as I could, given the circumstances.

I was eluding the police with the intent to leave the jurisdiction. I was an accused multiple murderer, violating the terms of my bond. Running scared, watching my back, hitching a ride on I-70 west, I was Louie on the lam, Louie without a clue. Somehow, it seemed right.

11

⸺⸺⸺ ◆ ⸺⸺⸺

The headlights of speeding semis and other overnight traffic illuminated the rear of the compact pickup that had stopped in response to my outstretched thumb. A bent and twisted license plate said something about Nebraska. The aluminum shell over the bed was covered with stickers and decals: hype for tourist traps from one coast to another— Russell Cave, Johnstown Flood Museum, Sunset Crater National Monument—and pithy homilies that preserved the wisdom of the road—"I Love My Country, It's My Government I Fear"; "Proud Parent of the Kid Who Beat Up Your Honor Student"; "I'm Ignernt and I Vote."

I jogged to the pickup and couldn't believe my luck. I had waited only a few minutes. I had stood near the freeway exit, unsure how exactly to go about escaping, and I had expected a siren and flashing lights any minute, and Tenorio to appear in his gravel-spewing police car, ready to drag me away from the shoulder of the highway. But instead, the pickup had responded almost immediately.

The passenger door swung open with a loud squeak and I peered into the cab. The thin edge of fear creased the base of my skull. What kind of person picks up a hitchhiker at one in the morning? I twisted my backbone in a sign of resignation. What kind of person hustles a ride from strangers at one in the morning? I was the guy accused of multiple sins, and in no position to judge anybody else.

The dark, mean face of Alton Enoch stared at me from behind the steering wheel, and I jumped back, my mind not accepting what my eyes had clearly seen.

"You want a ride or not? Come on, Pancho, I ain't got all night."

I looked at the face again, and Alton had been replaced with another black man who wore gray mechanic's overalls and a cap that looked as if it belonged on a train engineer's sweaty brow. He appeared to be about thirty-five, but he could have been fifty. I shrugged off my paranoia as a natural effect of the recent craziness. Any hint of self-chastisement because of my racial stereotyping slipped away as eagerly as I slipped into the cracked and spotted pickup seat.

I had to slam the door hard. The first time I shut it, it swung back open. He said, "That door is sprung, needs an extra push to shut." I exerted more force and it closed, but it didn't feel secure.

"Yeah, thanks. I sure need a ride. And it's Tony, not Pancho."

He laughed, shook his head, and turned up the volume on his all-night talk show. His right leg pressed down against the accelerator and we sped away from the exit.

The western half of Denver disappeared in the night, and I resisted looking backward. My ride was headed in the general direction of San Diego, and that had to be enough. I tried to get comfortable in the cramped quarters. The seat was littered with maps, fast-food cartons, cassette cases, and assorted wrenches. My side of the dashboard supported a wooden box that I assumed held more tools, and around my feet lay several inches of newspaper.

The radio cracked and popped, and occasionally faded out, but it was never turned off. A hyperactive talk-show host billed himself as Dr. Dan, the Information Man. His gig was trivial, irrelevant data about almost any subject, and occasionally he made an obscene remark about a politician, movie star, or sports idol. He took calls from depressed housewives, jittery security guards, gregarious truckers, and others who seemed to have nothing better to do in the early-morning hours than spew invective against "liberals, femi-Nazis, and the criminal elements." Some of the callers sucked on cigarettes, while others interrupted their harangues with drinks of what I took to be coffee.

My new chauffeur chuckled or nodded at the inane remarks of the good doctor. Eventually, a groggy announcer convinced Dan that he should take a break for the latest news headlines. A commercial came on and that gave the driver a chance to talk.

"They call me Perk, but the real name's Percival, Percival Jones, and I prefers Perry if anybody ever asked, but they don't. Goin' as far as Vegas; then I don't know what maybe Texas. The wife's supposed to meet me there—she's got relatives and spent most of the winter out there—but now that she knows I'm really comin', she may have already left. Wouldn't that be a kick?"

He sounded very earnest, so I took him that way. He turned and looked at me as if he expected me to respond.

"Yeah, if the wife left, I guess it would be a real shame."

"You know it, brother. Shame ain't the half of it."

He listened to Dr. Dan's spiel about the benefits of an all-around vitamin and mineral drink that had to be good, since Dr. Dan endorsed only those products he personally "got involved with." Then Perk asked, "Say, Pancho, what line you in? Do much travelin'?"

"I do what I can. Construction, mostly." I wanted to change the subject from yours truly to anything else. "And you, Perk? What is it you do, exactly?"

We might have been a couple of men talking over a beer or two, and that talk almost always included references to work. The night had enveloped us and the highway. Perk played with his brights and once in a while wiped something off the windshield with his wipers—I was never sure exactly what. I realized how wound up and tired I was when I started seeing highway spirits—fleeting gray images at the corner of my vision, or behind us when I turned my head; never enough substance to pin down, just an abstraction of memory, a mood from the past, out there in the barren west.

"Exactly's kind of hard to say. Little bit of this, little bit of that. Consulting work."

"Consulting, as in financial advice?"

"Well, sure. Financial, of course. But other stuff, too. I'm what you call an entrepreneur, and I help other folks get started in business. I'm a facilitator of fantasy, a doctor of dreams come true. I've done about everything, and I pass on my experience. For a price, naturally, but well worth it, my man."

"Goes without saying, Perk."

He was into it. He nodded his head excitedly and an urgent tone coated his words.

"People have ideas all the time, good moneymaking ideas. And that's about as far as it gets for most folks. One of the great problems with this country is its lack of imagination, and that's one thing I have in abundance! Ee-majj-in-a-shun! I know how to get the ball rollin'. I got the moxie to provide technical assistance, organizational know-how. I'm the man who can plan, the guy who can buy, and the dude who is shrewd. I've made more money for folks who never thought they'd amount to an anthill of rabbit shit. I see their potential before they even know they got any. Like you, Pancho. You're a good example of precisely what I am talkin' about."

"You're wrong there, Perk. I'm not interested in any get-rich-quick scheme. I've got enough going on right now."

"Oh, yeah, yes sir! You got plenty goin' on. New job. And I can see that you are an intelligent guy. A little quiet, and way suspicious. But you got smarts. Only thing is, look what you're doin'. Hitchin' across the country to work for another man. That ain't the way, man. Ain't the way."

He was throwing out some wormy bait, ever so casually, lightly, testing his line for nibbles. I had nothing better to do, so I played his game.

"Well, anybody would want to be their own boss and not have to answer to anyone. That takes money, and that's always been the stumbling block."

He smiled and bounced in his seat. He was a man who loved his work.

"You're right. To a point. A most important point, at that. Shit yes, you need money. But more important, you need a plan, and you'd be surprised that it don't usually take as much money as most people expect. For example, I worked with a fellow in Des Moines. Pleasant man, far as it went. Sold insurance for ten years, and that was it. That was all it ever would be. Thought he'd retire in another ten years, start collectin' his monthly pension check, what there was to it, and most likely go fishin' in the summer and hole up in the winter with his sour wife."

"But, let me guess, you worked out a plan for him, and changed his life."

"I hope you ain't laughin' at me, Pancho. Because that is exactly what happened. I found out he knew more about computers than many so-called computer jocks I've had to deal with. That's how he filled his time between claims and huntin' down new prospects. He had only seventy-five hundred in his savings account. But with that I got him set up on his own. Today, right this minute, he owns and operates Cornfield Computers in downtown Des Moines. Sells, repairs, and programs computers for most of the farmers in Iowa—who, by the way, all need computers nowadays, although most of them didn't know that until my friend talked to them. That was my idea. Opening the eyes of the customers to something that they needed and just didn't know it. I pointed out that he was a decent salesman. I helped him realize that his sales background and computer savvy were gold mines starin' him in the face. And that's what I can do for you. Just give me a chance."

"I don't think so, Perk. Like I said, I'm on my way to the coast for a new start. I can't change my plans now."

I was going to go into elaborate detail about why I had to walk away from guaranteed fortune and success, but he brusquely cut me off with a jittery wave of his hand. He reached across the seat and turned up the volume of his radio.

"The state police have announced that the woman's body found early this morning in Boulder Canyon appears to be that of Lisa Esch, missing since January. Lisa Esch was last seen the night before the murder of her brother, James Esch. Lisa and James Esch are the son and daughter of Denver's well-known and wealthy Greg and Beatrice Esch. Denver attorney Luis Montez has been charged in the murder of James Esch, and, it is expected, will also be charged in what appears to be the murder of Lisa Esch."

I quickly looked away from Jones and tried to focus on the details of the black mountains.

Perk let loose with a piercing stage whistle.

"Now that's a scary deal. Brother and sister, both killed. Must be for money. That's what it usually is, unless it's blacks killing each other. Sometimes I think white people kill themselves because they want each other's money, and black folks kill themselves 'cause we ain't got no money."

He didn't offer an explanation for brown-on-brown murder. Dr. Dan returned to blubber about his right to own any damn gun he wanted to, just like the Newnited States Constytushin guaranteed.

I only grunted at Perk's editorial. He wanted more.

"Kind of quiet, again, ain't you, Pancho? It's a long trip, man. You'll have to loosen up a bit."

I could think only of Lisa, and what her death meant to me. How could I talk about that? Chuey would have been routed by now. Larimer County sheriffs, Fort Collins police, and probably a few federal agents would have been all over my sister's farm the instant Tenorio and his pals had been alerted to the discovery of the latest body. Every cop in the western United States had to be looking for me, hoping to spot the crazy lawyer, eager to get a chance to bust one of the breed that paraded in the courts, pranced before juries and judges, and occasionally outwitted the DA and trashed months of hard police work. Charges would be filed against Roberta, Chuey, and Jesús. No, I didn't want to talk, but I had no choice.

"I'm tired, Perk. I've been traveling for days. Just come in from Kansas City. Haven't slept for some time. So, I'm out of it. And, yeah, it's terrible what people do to each other, for money or love or power or maybe just because it gets them off. It's bad, but there ain't a damn thing I can do, Perk. If you don't mind, I need some sleep. If you'd rather, you can let me off, and I'll sleep on the side of the road. Maybe your next passenger will be more talkative."

"Sheesh, man. Take it easy. You do need some sleep. Hope in the morning you ain't so cranky."

He settled in his seat against a cushion of wooden beads that was advertised on Dr. Dan's show as a back-saver. "A massage in every mile."

I closed my eyes. The wild cackle of Dr. Dan filled the pickup. Jones responded emotionally, alternating between enthusiastic approval and dark, silent disgust. Through the night and tedious miles, I knew that he studied me. His eyes inspected my clothes, face, and shoes. Any casual observer could see that I hadn't been on the road for days. He knew my name wasn't Pancho or Tony. And maybe he had tried to guess what it was that had bugged me, other than his contrived folksy demeanor.

I was in the middle of isolation and loneliness. I had an acute case of terror, and doubt. Perk and his radio were my world, but I didn't know him, couldn't confide in him, and didn't want to become involved in whatever it was that he called his life. Just get me farther west.

I didn't open my eyes until I felt the pickup slow down and maneuver off the highway and I heard the ring of a gas station's bell. My eyes had been closed, but I sure as hell hadn't slept.

The sun had not yet risen, and I didn't know the name of the small town in western Colorado. Perk gassed up and calmly accepted my ten dollars. I didn't know if he would still be waiting when I came back from the rest room, but ten bucks seemed like a cheap price for insurance. I did not want to stand alone on the highway as morning broke.

I used the toilet, stuck my face under the faucet, and tried to make something of the hair bent by Perk's uncomfortable front seat. When I did all I could with what the disinfectant-smelling rest room had provided, I emerged into the charcoal light of the last hour of night and looked for my ride.

Perk's pickup wasn't in the gas stall where he had stopped. I cursed. My mind tried coming up with options, plan B kind of thoughts, when I spotted the decals and the aluminum shell near the edge of the street, out of the way of red-eyed truckers who might also want some gas.

I opened the door and saw the gun in his hand at the same time.

"Climb in, Pancho. I've got a few questions. And since you seem to be the quiet type, maybe this'll help free your tongue. Funny, never met a lawyer who I had to encourage to start yappin'."

I climbed in. He tried to keep his gun pointed at me as he manipulated the steering wheel and gearshift. He had to concentrate on controlling the pickup, and he had to give the proper amount of attention to me. The gun moved up and down with each movement of the wheel, and I could almost see it flying across the cab after I had knocked it loose with a swift, deadly accurate kick. Almost.

He made it to a rest stop. Perk parked next to a couple of diesel-powered beasts, but they were silent and looked deserted. The drivers must have been sleeping. I had to think the worst about Perk. And it seemed as though I had been right when I had paused at his pickup's door, reflecting on the coincidence of race that lumped together Alton and Perk. I hate being proven right by the barrel of a gun in my face.

"What's up, Perk? Why the gun? I don't have anything worth robbing."

"I ain't a crook. You know that line? Honestly, though, Pancho, you haven't denied being a lawyer, and that radio spot about the dead girl's body made you more edgy than I seen anybody since my youngest told us she was pregnant. You're Montez, and you're runnin' scared, and I guess we got to find us the police. Ain't that about it?"

"I'd like to talk you out of that, Perk. There's more going on than what you hear on the radio."

"You'd have to be a hell of a talker. Number one, I haven't liked lawyers since I lost everything I had in a savings and loan and the guys who took my savings were all lawyers, and the lawyers who said they would get my savings back took whatever little bit of extra money I had left, and I ain't never got one penny of nothing. Number two, you sound like a dangerous man, a killer. Number three, you didn't exactly warm up to me. Fact is, you didn't want to take me up on my offer of a ride once you seen my pretty black face. Yup, you have to be a mighty fine talker."

I talked. Man, I talked. I told him the whole story, from the cold day I had a drink, and more, with Lisa until the night I walked away from my house. I explained the importance of *The People of the State of Colorado* v. *Esch,* and described the strange midnight wandering of Beatrice Esch. I explained Glory Jane's role and her ugly death, Strayhorn's too-coincidental accident, and how I found Jimmy's body.

Perk seemed amused by my oratory, but he didn't reveal whether he believed anything of what I had said.

"I liked that, Pancho. But, couple of things. Why you headin' west? And what you got against black people?"

"I don't have anything against blacks."

He smirked. I decided I had to offer an explanation about racial tension in the nineties.

"Look, I probably got as much racism in me as any non-black male who was raised in this country in the 1950s. I tried to deal with that long ago, but if there's any of it left, all I can say is that I apologize. I take people for what they do, not what they are. You don't have to believe me, but that's all I can say. If you thought I acted funny when I got in your pickup, you're right. I haven't hitchhiked since I was a teenager. I didn't know what to expect. And, don't laugh, but at first I thought you were Alton Enoch, Glory Jane's friend. My head tripped me up, something that happens once in a while."

He laughed a low, polite kind of laugh that gave him a few seconds to think about what I had said.

119

"You're good, Pancho. You might be all right in the courtroom."

I tried to keep with what I thought was my momentum.

"I'm going to the coast to try to track down the ex-cop, Martinez. He's the only lead I got. He was Strayhorn's partner. He must know what was going on with that crooked cop. And then he took off as soon as things began busting up. I feel like I need to find him and try to get some answers of my own. It's the wildest thing I've ever done, but then, I've never been charged with murder before."

"Yes sir, you're wild, I'll give you that. You won't make it out of Colorado, the way you been actin' with me. You're too suspicious, man, too jumpy. I'd like to believe you, I would, but you got some heavy baggage you're carryin'. At least two murders and that thing with the cop, on the take or not. They'll shoot you first chance you give them. I can't get into all that. I got my own burden. So you'll have to get out. I'll give you that. Then I'm goin' to go back to that station and call the cops. I'd start runnin' across that prairie if I were you." His gun emphasized his commitment to his plan.

I didn't blame him. There was no reason for him to get involved. I didn't agree that he had to call the cops. He could have dumped me and left it at that. I opened the door and inched my way out of the cab. I walked away from the pickup, my eyes on him as he kept his gun pointed in my general direction, until he lost sight of me in the predawn haze.

I jumped into a gully overgrown with wild grass and prairie weeds. I crawled a few yards, back toward the station. I peeked over the rim of the ravine and saw the shape of his feet walking by, a yard or so from my face.

I didn't think it through. I acted in reflex. I made a desperate move and didn't contemplate what it all might mean later, in a courtroom before a judge ready to pronounce sentence, or on the late-night news when breathless commentators would question how I had lost control—didn't I understand the consequences?

I scrambled up the short incline and tackled him. He cried out, not in pain but in frustration because he knew it wasn't finished. His arm circled my head in a wide oval, but the butt of his gun missed. I wrenched his arm behind his back and twisted it into a hammerlock. I covered his mouth with my free hand. He dropped the gun. I knocked him to the ground and held him down while I picked up the gun. He thrashed, rolled, and rocked like spit dancing on a hot stove, but I kept my grip.

"I'm sorry, Perk. But you didn't give me a choice. I'm going to California, and I guess you are, too. Let's go. You drive. I'll hold the gun."

"Son of a bitch! I knew you were trouble. Knew it. Next time I get my hand on that gun, I'll use it, Pancho. You can take that to the bank."

"Just drive, Perk. Nobody's getting shot. Not unless it's absolutely necessary. You know that line? And the name's Tony. Quit calling me Pancho."

12

◆

Something had happened to me. I didn't like it, but there it was. I added kidnapping to my list of crimes without as much as a twinge of regret. I had to do it. There was no other way.

Perk presented a major logistical problem. I couldn't possibly stay awake all the way to San Diego. I had to be alert enough to keep him under control. Somehow, I had to fit in eating, gassing up, toilets, and avoiding eager state police and curious small-town deputies. I wanted to ditch him, send him on his way to Vegas, but he knew my destination, and he was just the kind of guy who couldn't keep a secret.

I played with the idea of stealing his pickup. But I would have to hurt him to carry it off. I could have hurt him. My immediate problems could be solved by finishing him. I imagined, in finite detail, shooting Perk and leaving his body in the sage and sand of western Colorado. It sounded logical, coherent; there was an instant when it seemed easy, and reasonable. No more Perk, no reason to keep looking over my shoulder. Long before anyone found his body, I could breeze into San Diego, ditch the pickup, and get on with what I had to do.

I tried to stay away from that tunnel. I was riding a long, dark train, and whatever I did, I had to keep it on the track. I told myself, You're not the killer, Montez. I didn't understand why, but I wasn't as convinced as when I had faced up to Tenorio and Martinez.

In an effort to break free of the deranged thoughts, I ordered Perk to pull into a fast-food joint. From a drive-through speaker, he ordered breakfast. I kept the gun in his ribs to make sure he got the order right.

I felt better about him after I drank some coffee and choked down a greasy biscuit plastered around a piece of dry egg and sausage gristle.

The radio selections had been narrowed to country music, so I plunked one of his tapes into his player. The sexy voice of Marvin Gaye replaced the sexy voice of Dwight Yoakum.

I was dragged out—too wound up to sleep, but tired enough to drift off when I should have been concentrating on Perk. I felt flaky, disoriented. I must have slept, but I couldn't remember when. Perk looked bad, too. There was a high level of stress in the pickup.

Occasionally, Evangelina climbed into the pickup, but I shook her off, staying away from that piece of my history. There was enough going on without her complications.

"Look, Montez. This ain't goin' to work. This old truck is barely makin' it to Vegas. San Diego is too far for it, and for me. You bit off too much. You got to do better than this."

"Thanks, Perk. I didn't know that."

"Montez, I really don't like you. You got me prisoner in my own vehicle. You fucked up my arm bad. If the cops ever stop us, I'm sure they'll shoot me along with you and tell everybody that we was in it together, and everybody'll believe that. And it looks to me as though you deserve to be

locked up, so I won't really blame anybody if they com-
mences poppin' off shots at you. But I got to get out of this.
You got any ideas, since you the man with the gun?"

I was willing to deal. I had to. It sounded better than
killing the guy. I was as much his prisoner as he was mine,
and if we could work something out and eventually go our
separate ways, I thought we'd both be happier, and maybe
a bit wiser. Almost a win-win.

But there was very little I could offer. My only power over
him came from the gun, so I couldn't give that up. He didn't
seem like he'd get too turned on by a promise of free legal
services. It came down to what it always comes down to.
Although it seemed as if centuries had passed, I remembered the bottom line for the deals I'd had to negotiate in my
other life, as a lawyer. Maybe the color of the soul of this
particular soul man was green, as in money.

I had the remains of my bank account. The five thousand dollars was all that was left before the *caca* flowed over
the propeller blade.

"I'll buy a ride, and your silence. Three hundred for this
truck, and a grand for two days of silence. Then, if you feel
like you got to tell somebody, you're off the hook. I take all
the risks and you get the bread. The only thing is—"

"Yeah, I bet there's an only thing. Probably you want my
left nut for collateral."

"Perk! Don't we know each other better than that? I get
the truck, your cooperation, and your silence. And I'll leave
you someplace where you can't be found right away. That's
all."

A sliver of light flashed across his eyes, and he turned
his face too quickly. I needed something else.

"And, maybe, before that happens, you introduce me to
your wife when we pass through Vegas, so I know who she
is, just in case, you know, I ever have to look you up again."

"You motherfucker! You ain't gettin' anywhere near

124

Frances! I'll kill you, Montez, if you do anything, if you—"

"Hold on, man. Don't flip out on me. I'm negotiating. Trying to work something out. Look at it this way. If I really was as bad as your radio there has made me out to be, why would I be talking to you? I'd have dumped your dead ass a few miles back and shuffled off to California without even giving you a prayer. But that isn't me, Perk. That's what I'm trying to tell you. I'm going to clear all this up, one way or the other, or I'm going to get even with the people who have done this to me. I need some help, and I'll pay you for it, but I also need some time. If we don't agree, then it's one long ride to California, for both of us, and I got a bad feeling that only one of us comes back. It's your call. We deal or not?"

I had made everything up as I talked, and I didn't think I had anything like a plan, and I didn't expect anything from him. I counted on what I took to be my sincerity, but the words were an octave higher than usual, and I must have sounded a bit desperate, maybe a little crazy. But I urged him on, and I talked the talk and had him pull over so that I could walk the walk, and I even sang a song or two. Round about the middle of Utah, Perk and I had an understanding, an agreement.

A day and a half after we first met, Perk and I finally reached something like a destination. We found the mother's home in north Las Vegas. Perk pulled up to the crushed stone driveway, on the lip of a narrow, well-manicured stretch of scrubby lawn, healthy desert flowers, and blooming cactus barrels. He pressed the horn, then repeated his signal. We waited in silence.

Perk had agreed to accept five hundred for his truck and two thousand for his cooperation. The way we had it scoped out, I would dump him in a secluded area, tied up and far enough away from the road and rest stops that the odds would be against anyone finding him accidentally. I told him

I would call the appropriate authorities and let them know where he was as soon as I crossed the California border. After that, he could tell the cops whatever he wanted. The way I looked at it, I was the one taking all the chances—plus, it was costing me money. After he saw my stash, he was more open to the idea. I think he wanted to trust me.

A short young woman finally sauntered from the house. She wore neon blue shorts and a neon blue halter top, and sunglasses with bright blue plastic frames. She was brilliant in the daylight. Her skin, shiny as a new penny, and dark as an old one, reflected the sun, and she moved as effortlessly as a dust devil stirs the sand. Perk's face told me all I had to know about his relationship with his wife. When she leaned into the cab and smothered his mouth with her blue-colored open lips, I understood why Perk had chased her across half of America.

When she finally came up for air, she smiled at me, and I thought it was awful hot in Nevada, for it being so early in the year.

"Baby, this here's Tony, from Denver. I'm doin' him a favor. He has to get to California, and guess what this idiot wants. Wants to pay me to help him with the drivin'. He can't drive, never learned how. So I told him that I would help him out, if it's all right with you, of course. I'll get him to California, come back for you, and then we're off to Texas, like we planned. What you think, baby?"

Honey and sugar and syrup dripped from the neon lips. The words were something else.

"You must think I'm some kind of dumb ass, floozy bimbo if you think I'm letting you go to California without me. Percival, when I left you in Lincoln, I told you I was fed up with your running around the damn country without me. I was through with staying home, waiting for you until you get horny enough to come back through Nebraska. I quit that damn job at the Wal-Mart, and I expect you to take

126

care of me, now. You ain't going nowhere without me. And if you got to take this here Tony someplace, I guess we all got to go together."

Perk looked at me and grinned.

"She's a very stubborn woman. I guess if I go, she goes, too. Still interested in your deal?"

I had to think of something that sounded innocent enough to keep Frances from checking with the state patrol.

"Uh, Mrs., uh . . . Jones, uh, look. I'm in a real big hurry. I got a job waiting for me in San Diego, and I got to get there before tomorrow night. I need to get on the highway, and I thought I could make it profitable enough for Perk here that I could avoid the hassles of hitchhiking. But I really am in a big hurry."

"You wait five minutes. I'm ready to leave. I'll get my stuff and then we can all hit the road."

She pointedly removed her sunglasses. The Nevada sunshine danced around her face, and her smile had enough wattage to keep the Vegas strip going for an hour or two. She looked at me head-on, caught my twitching eyes with hers, and held them.

"But . . . something's bothering me. If you ain't got a job, until you get to San Diego, as you say, then, Tony, just how are you going to make this 'profitable' for my sweet, trusting Percival? And you ain't riding the bus, which could get you anywhere a lot faster than this old rattletrap, so, Tony, in just how much of a hurry are you really? Looks like something else is happening here, and one of you gentlemen is eventually going to tell me all of it. Ain't that right, Percival?"

Perk kept on grinning.

Frances put a different twist on the plan. She was not a party to whatever bonding process Perk and I had undergone during the long hours in his pickup. I couldn't hope that she would go along with the wild scheme, and I couldn't count on Perk to make her toe the line. I bet on his desire for the money. If he played along, he would still get paid. If he got in the way, he risked the money, Frances, and his life.

It took Frances maybe fifty miles to figure me out.

We had stopped at a gas station and I spent money on junk-food snacks, gas, and magazines for Frances. I seized the chance to talk to Perk while she freshened up.

He was okay, he said. If I didn't hurt Frances, he would talk her into going along with my plan—provided, of course, that I came across with the money. He needed time to explain it to her, he said. But it would be all right.

I felt like the victim instead of the perpetrator. Frances and Percival had me going—I just didn't know where. Or how much it would cost me in the end.

I wanted to let her know that I was okay, a regular guy. "How long you and Perk been together, Mrs. Jones?"

"Look, Tony, or whatever, you can call me Frances. We been having our thing for about ten years, right, Percival?" He nodded.

"That's great. Really nice." What else could I say?

She squirmed in the seat and I felt her thighs rub against my legs. I was pushed up against the ill-fitting passenger door, which I trusted less with each passing mile.

She took over the conversation.

"So you got a girl someplace? Back in—where was that, Denver? Got a lady friend waiting for you back home?"

"No, not really. Actually, I'm trying to make a new life out in California, and my girl, my fiancée, is waiting for me. She's been out there for a few months, waiting. I finally got it together to make the move."

"What's her name, Tony? What's she do?"

"Uh, Evangelina. She's a legal secretary. We been together for a long time. I hope we can finally tie the knot, or something meaningful, you know?"

She laughed. "Oh, hell, yes, I know exactly what you

mean. Good luck, mister. Ain't nothing better than a good loving relationship."

I withdrew into myself. I had lied about Evangelina, made up a story that didn't have one speck of truth, and I didn't know why. I tried to pass it off on my exhaustion, and the stress.

Frances moved on to more pressing subjects.

"Tony, or whatever your name is, what kind of mess you drag Percival into?"

"I've explained, Mrs. Jones. I'm on my way to a job. Perk was the first guy to pick me up. The two of you get the benefit of my urgent situation. That's all."

She shook her head emphatically. Bits of laughter escaped from her tempting mouth in occasional bursts.

"Man, you must think I'm dumb! What you say ain't so. We all know it. And it will be more comfortable for all of us as soon as you tell me the truth."

The laughter stopped. She nudged me and I thought she wanted more room. I couldn't move over. But it wasn't her fingers that poked my ribs. This couple had a good supply of guns.

"Jesus. What is this? Perk, tell her to cool it, or you blow the whole deal. Tell her, Perk!"

"Frances, what the hell you doin'? This guy could kill us all and not lose any sleep. He's wanted for a couple of killings back in Colorado. Frances!"

"He better tell me what this is all about, or we might have a little shoot-out here in this little tiny pickup truck. It could get real messy."

Perk responded eagerly. "Don't let your gun down, honey. I'll pull over, and we'll have a little talk with Mr. Tony. He's got money—a lot of money. Maybe this *will* turn out."

I was tired, fed up. I hadn't been thinking right for days. They pushed my final button, broke the old camel's back.

I swung my fist into her jaw as ferociously as I could in

the cramped space. I didn't have room for leverage, so the blow was not solid, or direct. But it did the trick. She turned her body to avoid my fist, caught the blow on her chin, screamed, and tried to aim the gun back in my direction. I grabbed her wrist, twisted, and slammed the gun against the dash. A shot echoed in the truck and the window next to my right ear shattered. A gust of wind whirled around the struggling woman and me. The sudden explosive gunshot had made Frances twitch, and she dropped the gun. It clattered to our feet.

Perk tried to help Frances. His instinctive response to the gunshot caused the pickup to swerve across the highway. We flew across the desert, dust and rocks flying around us, in the cab. Frances wrestled with me, trying to get the gun. I grabbed various body parts and held on while I bounced across the front seat. Perk was cussing a blue streak, trying to regain control.

We slammed into a small mound of earth. I was tossed from the cab through the suddenly open passenger door, which couldn't take it anymore. I clamped my jaws shut and bit into the inside of my cheek. I landed on my stomach, the wind knocked out of me, but I knew I was all right. I spit blood. The only other sounds were the hissing and regurgitation of the pickup as it drained some of its fluids. I gave myself a minute to catch my breath, then crawled to the side of the pickup and peered into the cab.

Perk and Frances had stayed in the pickup, and they were not as lucky as I'd been. Blood from a cut above Perk's head slowly dripped across his face. Frances was twisted across the seat. A bruise around her eyes from her impact with the dashboard already had darkened. They were both unconscious.

I didn't take time to think. I didn't do that anymore. I checked them to make sure they were still alive. Then I dragged them from the pickup, arranged them back-to-back behind the mound of earth, and tied them together with nylon rope Perk conveniently had stowed in his flatbed. Frances was mumbling and groaning, but she didn't wake up.

I left them the junk-food snacks, Perk's thermos of coffee and his jug of water, and the money I had promised. I claimed as mine the pickup, the title to the pickup, my backpack, and the guns. Frances had a nifty-looking switchblade in her purse, and I took that, too. She also had a wad of money, but I didn't touch it. At that point, the weapons seemed more important.

In a few minutes, I was back on the road, screaming toward the West Coast. I needed just a little bit of luck. If I got it, things would work out. If I didn't, I knew I would end up at a place I wouldn't like, but I would go there if I had to. The pickup had to last. Frances and Perk had to stay put, for a few hours at least. No one had to stumble on them. No cop needed to stop me, just for a routine check. No one had to question me about where I was going, what I was doing. No one had to fuck with me. Not anymore.

13

Perk's pickup sputtered and gave up its hearty ghost thirty miles from San Diego, in full view of the ocean. I abandoned it to the dirty gray sand, after having stripped it of all noticeable identification. Near a sign that warned motorists to watch for scampering undocumented immigrants, I raced across the highway. My mind and body acted as one, quickly and resolutely. There was no need for detailing plans or examining options.

I moved south along hidden paths and trails conveniently carved by refugees who scurried north. In the darkness, with my backpack secured around my shoulders, I stumbled across groups of people who avoided me as much as I wanted to stay away from them. We were midnight travelers, watching our backs, searching for a future that we believed in only halfheartedly, not sure why we hid like hunted animals. If I were stopped by *la migra*, the best that could happen to me was deportation, and that didn't seem too bad. The worst would be for the border cops to dig up my real name.

I made it to the outskirts of the city, and an all-night,

all-purpose supermarket where I found an old-fashioned telephone booth.

The phone rang twice in my ear, then stopped. A minute later, another call, one ring, then silence. My prearranged signal to Chuey was kind of hokey, and if Dad's line was tapped, the cops would know it was me. But it was all we could come up with before I hit the road. I had to have a way of getting in touch with him after he was back in Denver. No one thought they would spend much time in Fort Collins. When he got the phone calls, Chuey, or my father, if he was up to it, was supposed to wait for my call at the pay phone around the corner from my office, thirty minutes after the signal. Even if the police followed him, we thought we should have enough time to exchange messages.

I waited the half hour, trying to melt into the shadows of Pacific Beach. I punched in the number of the pay phone and waited for someone to answer. Almost immediately, Chuey's voice greeted me.

"Louie? This better be you. You owe me, again. I was off to a good time with Miriam—remember her? Then you called. I thought it was better for me to do the sneaking-around shit than the old man."

Chuey had stayed in Denver. Or a judge had limited his itinerary. There were a thousand details I wanted to learn, but I didn't have the time. I needed to deal only with priorities.

"Jesús okay?"

"Yeah, he's tough, *como siempre*. They harassed us for a few days, locked up the old man in the Larimer County jail, but they haven't followed through with anything. They finally turned us loose. He's weak, but solid. A stand-up guy, *firme*. He's there for you."

I cringed at the thought of Dad puttering around a cell, especially in his condition. One more brick piled on my overloaded back.

"I need a ride. I'm where I want to be, but no way to get around."

"Your squeeze, or ex-squeeze, whatever she is—she and Jesús worked something out. A car's waiting for you, parked near the handball court in Chicano Park. You know where that is? The murals, in the barrio. Don't ask me how she did it, but she said for you to use it and then, if you have to, bring it back here and leave it with her sister, Jenny. She'll pick it up one day. Assuming you don't wreck it first. She said you would recognize it, and she hopes you still got the key."

It was jingling on my key chain as Chuey talked.

"And Louie, *otra cosa.*"

"What?"

"She said not to call her. The car's one thing; she's something else. Whatever you did to her, you fucked up, man. *¡Ay, qué vato!* Keep your head on, Little Louie."

He hung up.

Pacific Beach looked interesting, and in the days before the Esch mess, I would have tried to find a bar with a heart, or a warm voice. But I couldn't stay. Everything now was "after Esch"; everything would always be that now.

I took a cab to the park, although the cabbie was reluctant until he saw my money. The barrio was miles away, in a different San Diego, and it wasn't difficult to see that Chicano Park at night was not his favorite destination.

In the cab, I pried loose the fragments of the Chicano Park story that I still carried from my days as a soldier in the Chicano movement. The battle for Chicano Park had remained with me as one of the shimmering memories of my youth, even though I was in Colorado when it had been fought. It had been my battle back then, too, back in 1970, because I was Chicano. I relished the joy of the fight and the eventual victory.

The people had won that battle, and the park stood as a

monument to the will of activists, organizers, and regular *gente.*

The barrio had been cut in half by Interstate 5. Politicians promised to preserve property near the east end of the San Diego–Coronado Bridge as a community park. One morning, the barrio was awakened to the sounds of a construction crew breaking ground for a California Highway Patrol station on the land that was supposed to have been saved for the park. The police station was designed to disperse the barrio, to cut out its heart and break it up.

The people of Barrio Logan had a different idea. They rallied around the bits and pieces of land under the bridge, fought the developers and politicians, and reclaimed their park. They ringed the work crews and stood as a human wall to stop the destruction of their space. Around-the-clock demonstrations stopped the bulldozers cold. San Diego proper had to back down.

The murals on the towering concrete pillars that braced the bridge honored the community, as well as dozens of Chicano heroes and myths. They had been restored over the years, and now they were more famous than the fight that had given them birth.

The irony of the bridge hadn't been lost on anybody. From a community of *taquerías, panaderías, segundas,* record shops, health clinics, liquor stores, and grocery stores—the essential components of any Latino neighborhood anywhere in the United States—it arched over the bay and landed near a golf course and a strip of high-end restaurants and nightclubs. The "village" of Coronado Bay had been built around the famous Coronado Hotel, hangout for presidents, movie stars, and assorted celebrities on their way to or from Mexico. Expensive homes were ringed by marinas and bike paths. The bridge was only a few miles long, but it covered a thousand miles of distance between Barrio Logan and Coronado Bay.

135

Martinez had found a way to link the two. His security outfit made money from the Coronado muckety-mucks, and I was sure his employees spent it in the barrio bars.

Evangelina's Honda Accord gleamed in a circle of moonlight. The cabbie turned into a parking lot near a group of young men who earlier in the day probably had been playing set after set of handball and who now gathered around customized cars and trucks, drinking beer. Bold mestizo figures and bright revolutionary colors flashed in the passing headlights and the fleeting moonlight. Concrete pillars served as easels for the majestic murals of Zapata, César Chávez, Cuauhtémoc, and a soaring Chicana liberated from the chains of machismo. Evie had a sense of cultural history I hadn't fully appreciated.

The driver hesitated. He had seen the men.

"You, uh, want me to stick around or something?"

"No, thanks. It's okay."

I handed him his fare and a healthy tip. I was out of the cab before he finished counting the money.

"It's your trip, man."

He drove away without waiting for a response.

I passed from the darkness into the glare of the park lights, and the stares of the low-riders. My wrinkled clothes and bleary eyes set me off from tourists, cops, and them. They didn't know what I was, and that made me at least interesting, and maybe untrustworthy.

The spot of light that framed the car made it easy for anyone to see me, and difficult for me to pick out details. Rough, loud talk carried freely in San Diego's night air, then echoed off the concrete overpass. The low-riders sounded agitated, mad. Maybe they didn't like strangers in their park after hours. Maybe they didn't like this particular stranger who hopped from a cab into a parked car that had no business in the parking lot. Low-rider car clubs in Denver could be innocent outlets for mellow, upright young men and women, or convenient covers for gangsters. I had never met a low-rider from San Diego.

I fiddled with my keys and the car door as I waited for the guy who had been picked for the job of checking me out. My palms sweated. I thought a hundred men gathered at the other end of the park.

"*Orale, viejo.* What's up?"

A short, sweaty Chicano in a shiny nylon jacket carelessly carried a can of beer. He flashed a bright smile, but his movements were wary, defensive. He waved to his buddies, a signal that so far everything was cool. I read the flowery script on the back of his jacket: *Uniques Car Club.*

"Hey. Picking up my friend's car. She had to leave it here earlier. Taking it back for her. Got the keys right here."

The door opened and I slid into the front seat. The guy quickly stepped up to the door and held it with his free hand. I had the choice to slam it on his hand or let him finish what he had been sent to do. I settled back into the Mexican blanket Evangelina had draped across her upholstery.

He looked in the car, scanned the backseat, then stared at me.

"You be careful, man. There's a lot of punks, troublemakers trying to fuck up our park. We watch out for them. We don't want any bullshit, from them or the Man." He paused, sipped his beer. "But you know that. Take it easy, bro."

He was gone. I started the car and eased out of the parking lot. The Uniques eyed me every inch of the way.

Somewhere in San Diego, Ben Martinez waited for me to find him. He had to know that I was on the loose, and if my suspicions about him were right, he also knew that I would be looking for him. I wasn't much of a threat to him—hell, he would be a hero if he broke my back—so I didn't expect him to run or hide. But he would be waiting, and that made him more dangerous for me.

My research back in Denver had given me the address and phone number for Big M Investigations, as well as background information. Big M was John Martinez's baby. Ben's older brother had organized the operation a dozen years ago and soon worked it into an efficient and useful enterprise for lawyers who dabbled in personal injury, criminal defense, or messy domestic matters. John's hard work paid off and he plugged into the lucrative continuous games enjoyed by Southern California's rich and famous—infidelity, business double cross, and family scandal. Ben fell into the business when John decided to turn his attention to other endeavors, the exact nature of which, I couldn't learn. Although Ben Martinez played up his sudden and abrupt retirement as his chance to cash in on big bucks, it was too coincidental for me. Ben left Denver without clearing his dead partner's name, or even trying to finish pinning the rap on me.

As Jesús might say, Don't trust a rooster who sleeps while the fox prepares breakfast.

I found a motel. I didn't have much of anything left. Time, money, energy—all were in short supply. I was drained, played out. My clothes were as limp as my sex drive, my mouth tasted like a poker-game ashtray, and my brain felt like a soggy pretzel floating in a pool of stale beer. It was time for sleep.

14

The hate I had for Ben Martinez plagued my sleep. I didn't think he was a killer, just a chicken-shit who knew I had been framed, did nothing about it, and probably had something to do with it.

In my exhausted torpor, I slipped into nightmare visions tinged in shades of iron gray and khaki brown. Frayed autopsy pictures of Jimmy Esch and Glory Jane Jacquez flapped in the desert wind. A cadaverous, cackling *mojado* pointed toward the mountains, where a cloud of red dust spiraled from the hooves of two giant animals. Martinez and Ug Tenorio chased me across the Great American Desert. Dressed in crisp shiny blue cop outfits with brilliant golden badges indifferently pinned to the brims of their cop caps, and madly waving huge wooden batons, they rode ugly, sweating horses that melted into an image of a flying late-model Chevrolet sedan—the type of car Strayhorn had died in. Tenorio drove, Martinez screamed from the passenger seat, and in the rear sat Perk and Frances and Glory Jane and Jimmy Esch, and squeezed into the corner perched an effervescent, smiling Lisa. I saw all of this, although I ran for my life before the thundering machine, across cactus, sand, and slot machines. And there was something else about the car. Blood and gore splattered against the rear window and I could see that it came from the horrible gash across Lisa's throat. I stopped running. I faced Strayhorn's death machine. I stood in the Nevada night, mesmerized by the car and its ghoulish occupants. I waited for it to overrun me.

I jerked awake and twisted upright. I was half-asleep, drenched in sweat and darkness, and I didn't know what city I was in, or what I was doing in the strange bed. When I finally realized I was in a San Diego motel, I knew I would not sleep again that night.

I waited in Evie's car at six in the morning for Ben Martinez to show his face.

Big M Investigations was housed in a squat one-story building surrounded by an eight-foot wooden fence. Numerous cameras, lights, and warning signs were positioned along the perimeter. A wide, swinging steel gate provided the only entrance to Big M's parking area. It was locked but unmanned. The gate's guard hadn't started his shift yet, although I didn't doubt that a night person roamed Big M's halls and offices, or sat staring at a wall of monitors fed by the cameras.

A large sign arched over the entrance. Big M's logo consisted of a ferocious-looking dinosaur standing guard outside the entrance to a prehistoric cave. The monster wore a cap that had the words *Big Emmett* above the bill. He clutched a semiautomatic rifle. A couple of dead or grievously injured cavemen sprawled at the feet of the dinosaur. Not subtle, but effective.

Big M had an image to maintain—a high-tech, professional security service that provided top-notch bodyguards, effective and expensive home and business security systems, and the best snooping in Southern Cal. That kind of presentation required a fence and a gate and a guard on the outside of the office, and probably bulletproof glass, impressive computer systems, and more guards on the inside—where Martinez was untouchable. I had to get to him before he made it into his building.

A little after eight, Ben Martinez arrived. He drove an expensive black automobile with gold trim. The tinted windows prevented me from seeing him, but when the driver's window electronically dropped and he showed his face to greet the guard, I recognized him. The guard laughed and said something to Martinez that made him laugh, too. In a few seconds, Martinez was behind the gate, and safe.

I sat in the car for the entire morning. My company was a mixture of self-indulgent memories and calculations. Evie and I had made love in this cramped backseat, where I had just tossed an empty Styrofoam coffee cup and a tourist's map of San Diego. There were days when it had been enough for us to drive around Denver in this car, exploring places we had no reason to visit except that we were in love and that's what we did when we were in love—Observatory Park, Chatfield Lake, the back road to Brighton.

I tried to focus.

Customers came and went, and others, who wore what I took to be the Big M uniform, showed up at different hours, presumably reporting in from different jobs. Occasionally a police car turned into the business property. Big M and the cops must maintain a good working relationship.

I concentrated on invisibility.

Near one in the afternoon, when my rumbling stomach would not leave me alone and I had decided to look for some quick food, Martinez's black car whipped through the open gate and out into the street. I fumbled with the ignition as I tried to keep him in my line of vision.

I followed him for several miles along the freeway before he exited. He drove for a dozen more blocks, then parked at a marina restaurant. He strolled in, casually, all the time in the world.

That did it for me. Martinez had it made in this town that was so close to the Mexican border that, from the right angle, a person could see the smoking Tijuana dump. He was into a good business, a good car, and now a good restaurant, and the only conclusion I could make was that whatever was left of my life hinged on what he would reveal. I had no business, no car, and I doubted that I would ever eat in a good restaurant again. We were both Chicanos. We supposedly shared a culture, some kind of tradition. Deep down, we were brothers. And I knew that if he didn't give me what I wanted, we would end up as just one more statistic. Another act of violence between two Mexican-Americans. Another chapter of the American tragedy acted out by bit players for the greater audience, with whom we would never sit.

I watched and waited again.

He emerged an hour and a half later, his arm draped around a woman dressed in Southern California affluent grunge. She politely kissed him on the cheek, then waited for the valet to bring her car. Martinez climbed into his own ride.

I had to act. I waited for him to get back on the freeway. I timed my move as best as I could remember the freeway exits and entrances. I pulled in behind him and inched as close as I could, pushing Evangelina's car to keep up with his. He saw me as a stupid tailgater and tried to speed up. He tried evasive tactics that he probably trained his men to use. His best bet appeared to be simply to use his car's power and leave me in the wake of high-priced gasoline fumes.

Before he lost me, I pumped the accelerator for all it was worth. I aimed at the Big Emmett decal on Martinez's bumper. I nicked his rear fender and opened a minuscule gash in the shiny surface of his car. He swerved into the outside lane. I almost lost control of Evie's car. The Honda savagely jerked to the right and it was touch-and-go for a few seconds before I felt like I had it back in my hands. Other drivers flipped us off, shouted at us as they gripped their steering wheels, some in panic, most in anger. He moved back into my lane, but I had dropped back. I slowed down and exited at my first chance. I gambled that Martinez had been in California long enough to know that he had to do something to me. He couldn't pass up a chance to bust my ass, and that meant he would double back as soon as possible.

I waited near the exit. He didn't disappoint me. California drivers obviously take their driving very seriously.

He sped by, dented fender and all, then, a few yards beyond the shadow of Evie's car, he stopped abruptly. Tires cried and black skid marks bruised the gray pavement. His car sputtered spasmodically, in rhythm, I suspected, with the driver's anger.

I made a show of turning quickly into an alley. He followed and I led him away from the freeway, away from traffic and the curious.

The empty lot appeared like a mirage and I had to use it. An expanse of blowing trash and salty, cracked soil offered the space I needed. I stopped and waited for him in Evangelina's car.

The black beauty roared up into the lot and then savagely braked. Martinez jumped from the car and ran to me. His face was twisted in anger.

"What the fuck do you think you're doing? You stupid son of a—"

Frances's .38 pointed at his belly.

"I'd think you'd know better than to get embroiled in a traffic altercation, Ben. They can be dangerous."

"Well, well, well." He stepped back from the car. "Look at

this. Louie Montez. I should have known. Only a crazy motherfucker would do what you just pulled on the freeway. And you are crazy, aren't you?" I didn't think he wanted an answer.

"You and I need to talk. So, let's get out there in the open, where any nosy neighbors might see us. I think we'll be less suspicious. Try not to forget that I got this gun, and, like you said, I'm crazy, crazy enough to use it, if I have to. Don't make me, Martinez."

He stepped back another yard and I eased my way into the sunlight. The gun was hidden from a witness's view by my jean jacket, but Martinez could see enough of it to keep the threat running around his freaked-out imagination. I also had Frances's switchblade tucked in my pants pocket. I was enjoying myself. For a change, I was on the dishing-out end of trouble.

"You don't look so good, Montez. You look like shit. I guess running to save your dumb ass doesn't suit you."

I punched him in the stomach and he fell to his knees. The gun was about an inch from his nose.

"Ben, you may have noticed. I'm not the same patient, easygoing guy I used to be. You keep fucking with me and I'll shoot off your big toe, just to make a point. How does that suit you?"

"Goddamn you! If you didn't have that gun, I'd . . ."

"What would you do? Not a damn thing. Here, come and get me." My empty hand appeared from my jacket. The gun stayed in my pocket.

He looked at my hand, then at my pocket. His lower lip trembled a bit. His eyes told me that he was really thinking about rushing me, trying to figure out how long he would have before my fingers wrapped around the trigger again, and whether he would be quick enough to knock me down before I got off a shot. Martinez wouldn't take the chance. I acted as though I knew that.

"You're not going to do anything, Ben. If you had stayed in Denver, I might think more of you. But you dropped your balls off when you came out here. You gave up on your partner, on the Esch case, and me. You screwed me, man. Now, sit down and let's talk."

I tapped his chest with my open palm, and he fell back on his butt, in the dirt. I bent down on one knee, my hand back on the gun, and glared at him. He looked tired, resigned, and a bit bored.

"You paid off Strayhorn. And you probably killed him, and Esch, too. He was a bad cop, and he tried to take me down with him. I guess he got what was coming to him. And now you want to kill me. You're an animal, Montez. A wild, demented animal."

"We can talk about my mental state later. I don't have a lot of time, so let's get on with it."

He stared at his shoes and said nothing. I wanted to smash his head with the butt of the gun, and I wanted him to talk without me having to do anything. I tried a story.

"You know, Ben, not long ago my father told me about a poker game he had once, with the devil, or somebody like that. I wasn't sure what it was all about, but the story sure stayed with me. It's been bugging me ever since I heard it, and I couldn't piece together why. I had time on the road to think it over. Who knows what it meant for my father, but I think I know what it means for me."

His eyes moved upward to my face. I swept my arm in a wide circle that enclosed the horizon from the ocean to the city.

"This is all a game, Ben. A game with only one guaranteed outcome, and for some of us it happens quicker than others. But we all have the same finish waiting for us, no matter how we try to stack the deck. My time may be up, but I'm not willing to cash in, not yet. I could be bluffing, or not.

145

But I will find out what the hell is going on, Ben. On that, you can bet."

I quit talking. My silence seemed to bother him as much as my rambling.

He said, "What is it? What do you want?"

"One of the things about the Esch case that nagged at me was the arrest, Ben. It was too pat. Alton Enoch was a veteran con. He knew too much to drive through a red light. Especially when he was holding and his passengers were fucked up. He wasn't high—that was clear. Yet he practically invited the cops to stop him. At least, that's the story you told in court."

"Come on, Montez. We had a tip. Everyone knew that. The traffic stop was our cover. But it was a good bust. We had very reliable information. And if it hadn't been for Strayhorn's flip, the case would have stood on its own. He earned your money. I'll give you that."

"I've gone through that with you. Look, it's just you and me out here. No judge, no Tenorio, no jury. I'm telling you, I didn't buy Strayhorn. If he changed his testimony for money, it wasn't mine. Someone else got to him."

He lifted his head for a second, but whatever it was passed, and then he shrugged, as though it didn't matter. He didn't care anymore about the Esch case and his dead partner. He'd left that behind and I was just an ugly reminder, a pest that he had to deal with only because I held a gun. I kept at him.

"And I also believe that you and Alton Enoch are old friends. If anybody flipped, it was him. He'd been your snitch for years. I could see that in the files Ybarra pulled together. Enoch's handle was Juju, magic. For years he'd played the role of the untouchable, the hood with major pull downtown. When he walked away from one of Strayhorn's busts, it confirmed that he did have influence with the right people, or, in your case, the wrong people. Everyone thought Strayhorn had cut a deal with Juju years ago, but you were the one—Strayhorn's partner, the straight arrow, ambitious cop who hid behind Strayhorn's dirty shadow. Enoch fed you information, and you protected him. And one day he fed you his old pal, Jimmy Esch."

He spit in the dirt and looked away from me and the barrel of the gun.

"I never did anything illegal, Montez. I was a good cop. I used scum like Enoch to get other scum, like Esch. I never lied in court, I never took a bribe, and I never murdered anybody. Up until this minute, I wouldn't have said the same about you. I would've sworn that you bought Strayhorn, and killed Esch, too. You're a prick who would do anything to get over in court."

I inched forward, waiting for the words that would mean I had to smash the gun across his face. His jawbones stretched and tightened against his cheeks.

"I thought you were a greedy shyster who killed to protect his ass when it got stuck in your plan to get at the Esch money. Now, I'm not so sure. And I can't say I care."

I cared. And that made all the difference in the world.

We had a good discussion, one of those conversations that lingers afterward because of all the meaningful insights and clever dialogue. When I left him, I felt better about San Diego, about Percival and Frances, even about the long trip back to Colorado. Funny how one person can affect another person's life that way. ¿No?

The scene with Martinez bothered me, later, when I sat in a lumpy chair in the motel room, oblivious to the noisy TV. I hadn't had a drink in weeks, not until that night. But I surrounded myself with a bottle of bourbon, a six-pack of beer, a bucket of ice, and water from the sink, if I needed it.

147

I didn't get drunk, but the liquor moved me from uneasiness about my macho bullshit with Martinez to downright remorse.

I realized that I had been watching the final innings of a sloppy San Diego Padres adventure. I had been a man who enjoyed baseball, who planned his schedule around minor-league doubleheaders and who had hoped to spend most of the summer gripping a ballpark hot dog and a beer, my eyes wide open to the marvel of major-league baseball in Denver. That had all slipped by me. Back home, the new Rockies had created a wave of fan hysteria. Every game in the uncomfortable baseball stadium had been sold out since opening day. The team was scheduled for its first tour of the West Coast in another month, and the hapless San Diego Padres were first in line, then the Dodgers. I had missed the home games, and I was too early for the historic first Rockies game in Jack Murphy Stadium. I blamed Martinez for that, too.

What had happened to me?

Sometimes three beers hit harder than ten, and I fell asleep in the chair before I came up with an answer.

Another beautiful balmy West Coast morning cushioned my junior hangover as I chugged off in Evie's car. I had a headache, and a slight case of the blues—nothing major. My only goal was to put as much distance between San Diego and me as soon as I could. I struggled with the temptation of calling Evangelina, of talking with her and maybe trying to see her before I left California. The struggle ended, and in a few hours I was in Arizona, and all she meant to me was contained completely in the automobile I was driving back to Denver.

15

Ybarra took my call immediately; then he quit on me. That was his first reaction.

"I can't represent you, Montez. I'm going to withdraw from your case. You've blown the only chance you ever had. There's no way I can do anything for you. This is it."

And so on and so forth. In the end, he stayed with me, although he insisted he didn't want to know where I was or where I had been. He would do what had to be done as my lawyer, assuming my case didn't end with a bullet from a police Special.

"Louie, you have to turn yourself in. That's the only thing I can advise. I can't condone your continued breaking the law, and I can't aid and abet. I should notify the cops that you contacted me. You violated your bond conditions, and they intend to charge you with Lisa's murder. It's just a matter of time. If they bring you in, you might as well expect never to see daylight again. There's no way a judge would let you wander around loose after your little vacation. Whatever you're up to, it won't work."

That was probably a clue that he wanted to know what I was trying to do, but I didn't bite.

"You should know that you do have some friends. At least, people who have offered to help. Jenny Rodriguez, you know about her. She calls every other day, worried about you, wanting to help. And Janice Kendall, she's still with you. Actually, a couple of lawyers have let me know they'll do what they can. Kendall, and your old pal Dave Padgett. I think he's filled with regret that his referral opened up this mess. I like that guy. He might do us some good. That's about it, though. After twenty years in this town, I hoped that you would get more support from the legal community. *Ya sabes,* that's the way it goes."

I hadn't expected any support. I thought I was doing pretty good with the so-called legal community, considering the context. I let his words dangle on the end of the quiet telephone line. He returned my silence with a time-honored lawyer tactic.

"And by the way, I sent you my latest bill. The firm insists that I keep sending you statements, even though I know it's a waste of time. You've gone over the edge. I wish you well, pal."

Then I went to work on him. I told him I had some hunches. I gave him part of the story of Ben Martinez, and the colorful history of Alton Enoch, without letting on that I had heard the juicy stuff firsthand from Martinez. He didn't want to, but eventually Ricardo responded. He warmed up to my case again, and did some thinking out loud about his defense strategy.

"If we can get a jury thinking that Enoch set up Esch, it's only a hop, skip, and a jump to plant a doubt in their minds about motive, and opportunity. If Enoch thought he was about to get burned, that he was the target of his own double cross, then it's more than reasonable to think that he acted in character, and took care of his buddy the way any self-respecting small-time hood would do. It's a thought, Louie. We'll work on it."

I had my own agenda and I pumped him for information that would help me with it. His job was in the courtroom. Mine was out in the streets and alleys where Lisa, Jimmy, and Glory Jane had faced their savage end. We had all been at the center of a dark unknown force that was still out there, and only I had survived.

I took on more guilt. Above the silent recriminations, I nodded my head to Ricardo's litigation tactics, knowing that it would never come to that.

As far as I was concerned, the only bit of real news from Ricardo was that Arnold Mansfield had never heard of Jimmy Esch until he read a copy of Judge Bernstein's decision.

I rented a room from a dusty old man who rented out dusty old rooms in a drafty three-story house near downtown, not far from the Capitol. The tenants were the mix I expected in a cheap apartment house. My neighbors included women always about to regain custody of their kids, men with prison pallor, and brooding young toughs who played the loudest music and scowled every time they saw me. My room became the base for my operations.

The money picture was close to desperate, and I didn't expect to remain invisible to Tenorio for much longer. And, although I tried to avoid it, I had to admit that I was becoming more and more afraid. The killer had to want me as much as I wanted him. As I stared out the smeared window of my room that overlooked noisy Colfax Avenue, I didn't doubt that he was looking for me. The issue had to be forced, and I would either save my hide or go down.

I had only a few days. Tenorio knew me, and my family. I understood his need to bring me in. It had to do with old insults, real and imagined, and youthful, ignorant competition. My eventual arrest was just another step in the process we had instigated years before, and I accepted that. But Ug

151

would also understand. He had to expect me to stay in Denver, where I could watch over Jesús. Tenorio waited for my mistake.

In the isolation of my room, I stared into the face of a primeval contradiction. Time was precious because I could sense it running out. It slipped away in bunches of minutes before I recognized them for what they were. It was gone before I had used any of it. But time was all I had. My rent was paid for a week, I ate once a day, read the newspaper, studied the file on my case that I had carried across the Southwest, and watched the street from the room's window. And so, time became irrelevant.

I spied on the prostitutes as they hustled themselves, but I was never tempted. Sulking, ugly young men hurried up and down the street, on the way to a connection, or a party, or maybe a job. They looked like people who hated my people, and they made the street uncomfortable. Shabby, forlorn panhandlers searched trash bins and inspected discarded cigarette butts. I pitied the crackheads who did what they could, usually with malevolence, to stave off their inevitable miserable ends. The city generated a convenient frame for my state of mind.

I had to act, and yet I couldn't. My brain focused on the Esch family, and my heart cried out for revenge, but my body stayed in the room.

I controlled light in the room by moving the heavy opaque curtain. In the mornings, bright yellow filtered the dust and sprayed the walls with ironic hope. By afternoon, I had closed the curtain and the room turned into a gray box. The overhead lightbulb illuminated the table where I sat hunched over the documents that recorded my legal battles. I scoured the papers for a clue to my salvation.

I no longer thought of myself as a lawyer, or a worn-out, middle-aged male, or a Chicano adrift in an uptight, vindictive Anglo world. I was a core of something without an identity. I was a fever I felt for the first time in the Nevada desert when I trussed up Perk and Frances and then discarded them as though they were used-up litter. The fever's tempo had sped up in an empty lot in Southern California when I threatened Martinez and saw him flinch in recognition that I would use the gun if necessary.

From that room, where no human voice interrupted my silence and no human touch disturbed the patterns of sameness on which I had come to rely, the fever glowed with the beat of my heart. It reached out and searched.

The night I made my move was no different from the others I had spent in that room. I wolfed a fast-food sandwich and four cups of coffee. I walked back to my room, where I picked up my denim jacket and my gun.

I drove Evangelina's car, for the first time in three days, south on University Boulevard to the exclusive Esch neighborhood. The trip from California had not done it any good. It sounded coarse and weak, in a way that reminded me of my father's recent brush with death. The front end swayed with a distinct right-angle twist that pushed my driving skills to their meager limits. My highway adventure with Martinez had partially disabled Evangelina's auto, and flying across the Southwest in my race to get back home had made it age prematurely. I didn't know how I would explain it to Evie, but I didn't dwell on my transportation problems.

I hid the car in the darkness of tree shadows. Were the cops watching the house? The street was quiet and isolated. The gate across the Esch driveway was obviously locked, but someone had added a heavy chain and a padlock. No lights were on in the house. I leaned against an old evergreen that sprawled outside the Esch yard. I waited for something to happen.

The idea of breaking into Beatrice and Greg Esch's home had first come to me on the drive back from California. I had convinced myself that I needed to confront the remnants of

153

the Esch family. That family had been at the root of my troubles, and I didn't know why. Jimmy Esch had been just another client, until he turned into my nightmare. Beatrice Esch had been intent on driving a spike through my heart, but she enjoyed it too much. She was more than an hysterical mother. And she had visited Juju, Alton Enoch, at a time and in a way that had no connection to her Cherry Hills Village surroundings. Ben Martinez had had some of my answers, and I suspected that Beatrice Esch held a few more.

I couldn't get to the Eschs without forcing an introduction. They wouldn't meet over a cinnamon roll at the coffee shop in the Cherry Creek Mall, and if I turned myself in to Tenorio, I doubted that they would stop by during visitors' hours at the county jail. I had to go to them, without any interference from the cops, or Enoch.

The headlights lit up the gate before I knew a car had pulled into the driveway. It was a quiet, expensive car. The Dobermans rushed to the gate like the good sentries they were, where they unleashed a few barks and howls. They quieted and ran back to their pen on the far side of the house when Greg Esch emerged from the car. He unlocked the chain and climbed back into the driver's seat, without opening the gate.

The night paused around me. I crouched under the pine branches, ready to move. The car purred insolently. The city that surrounded us had disappeared, and enigmatic time had ceased functioning for me.

The gate swung open and at that same instant lights went on in the house and along the driveway. The car quickly passed the swinging gate's doors. Almost immediately, they began to close. I jumped from under the tree into the yard, then rolled across the lawn, away from the lights. I lay under a juniper with tough old branches and needles that poked at the intruder. The gun dug into my hip.

154

I heard a thump and felt a vibration along my spine. The thump continued until I realized it was my heart; then I didn't notice it anymore. One of the lights in the house went out, giving me a dark path to the wall of the house. I crawled to a window ledge, where I hugged the ground, fear suddenly paralyzing me. It is no good, I thought. I'll end up arrested, or dead, shot by the enraged Beatrice Esch—it will be Beatrice, not Greg. But I couldn't retreat. I had no place to go, except the room, and now that I had escaped its hold, I had to act. I convinced myself I was my only hope, as slim as that might be.

The burger-joint coffee had backed up on me, and although I wanted to ignore it, my bladder was full and needed emptying—one of the results of years of drinking too many before-court cups of coffee and after-court bottles of beer. I stood and stretched against the house. The zipper screeched, and the flow of piss splattered across the Esch homestead. I worried about dribbling on my shoes until I accepted the wretchedness of my position. Even so, I shook myself so I wouldn't spot my pants.

I was moving along the exterior of the house, searching for an opportunity, when the dogs' barking tore open the night. I froze, but I knew it was no good. They were running toward me from the other side of the house. My real surprise was only that it had taken them so long to pick up on me.

I ran to the back of the house. The Dobermans snarled and yipped, not at me but at the thought of what they would do to me when they caught me.

A light switched on in a room near a side door. Greg Esch ran out into the night, brandishing his own pistol. I heard Beatrice holler, "Greg, get back here! Don't go out, you idiot! Shut the door!"

One of the dogs had caught up with me. He snipped at my feet, and I could feel his teeth snapping around my ankles. I sensed him ready to leap at my back.

I jumped over three narrow concrete steps and barreled into Greg Esch before he got a fix on where I was coming from. We crashed through the open door and into a wooden chair. The dogs scrambled up the short stairway. I kicked the door shut as I wrestled the gun away from Esch. The dogs clawed at the door, their whimpers of disappointment replacing their snarls.

Esch lay on the floor, dazed from my rude entrance. Beatrice Esch raced into the room. I turned the gun on her.

"Stop! Don't do anything! Stay right there. Don't move!"

She stopped and stood almost at attention. Her hands went to her mouth as soon as she recognized me. Her eyes moved around the room as she tried to think of something to do. It was that look, that sense she broadcast of preoccupation with figuring out what needed to be done, even in the midst of chaos, that made me think of Lisa. They were so similar, in looks and mannerisms, that I was more spooked by Mrs. Esch than I had been by her dogs. I stood up and tried to take control before Beatrice devised a way to deal with me.

16

Beatrice and Greg huddled in the shadow of a massive oak entertainment center. Blond shelves conspicuously exhibited too many CDs, cassettes, videos, laser discs, and magazines. The room must have served as an all-purpose family center. I did a quick survey and I saw, scattered from one wall to another, plastic lawn darts resting against a wall, near a set of rusty horseshoes; a stack of board games waiting for relatives and the holidays; badminton equipment in an unopened box; a stained ironing board; photo albums with curled pages; a collection of ceramic penguins; a family of handblown glass swans; and, finally, somehow ominously, a framed picture of Jesus Christ pointing at his flaming heart. Christ graced the mantel of a dead fireplace.

My father kept the same picture near the shrine he had constructed in honor of my mother, whose portrait hung near the Sacred Heart. It felt very uncomfortable, but I had found something in common between the Westside and Cherry Hills Village.

What had once been red hair had faded to a mellow shade of orange-yellow, and the artificial tightness of Beatrice's facial skin betrayed an extensive use of the skills of a plastic surgeon. And yet, I found her hard quality attractive, in much the same way I had gravitated to Lisa. Beatrice was short, intelligent—and dangerous. My first impression of Mrs. Esch had also been my first impression of her daughter, and if I had acted on that impression, I never would have been in Lisa's house the last night she was alive—and certainly not in Beatrice's home with a gun in my hand, trying to rein in the hostile and frightened parents. These thoughts scurried around my slightly loose brain as I fumbled for my next move, now that I had made it inside the Esch residence.

Greg Esch leaned on his wife. His skinny frame melted into hers. I didn't expect him to do anything on his own. He would follow her lead. Everyone in that room realized that his silly act of bravado had made it easier for me.

"You here to finish the job, Montez? Too many loose ends so you thought you'd take care of us the same way you killed my son?"

She didn't stumble over the words. Her voice was strong, without a hint of the pain she must have had over the death of her children—the same pain she had so eloquently expressed to the TV cameras filming her interview with Wanda Higgins.

"Mrs. Esch, no matter what you think, I'm not responsible for what's happened to your family, or to you. I'm trying to help myself."

The brief interchange of their eyes offered me nothing. It could have been fear, surprise, or shock.

She pushed Greg away with the same impatient attention that a mother uses when she straightens her little boy's clip-on tie and pats down his cowlick before they enter church.

Quietly, she tried to deal with me.

"You're a fool. You break into our home, attack us, hold us hostage. You're going to be sadly disappointed if you

158

think this insanity will help you in any way."

I stopped her before she could get in another word.

"Damn! I'm at the point where I almost don't care what happens, Mrs. Esch. I don't have the time or patience for any more crap. Right now, this minute, anything that happens outside this house is out of my control. But what happens in this house is pretty much up to me."

They backed up instinctively. I had come on too strong.

"Oh hell! Please. Try to listen to me. I'm here for the truth. It may not be enough to keep my ass out of prison, but it's all I've got to keep me going."

A long, deep sigh slipped out of her. Her body seemed to shrink even more, and for the first time I noticed a slump in her shoulders. When her hands began to shake, she grabbed the back of a chair. Her head drooped. Tears bubbled in her eyes and slipped down her made-up cheeks. Greg placed his arms around her and brought her back to his side. He finally said something.

"Isn't it enough that you've ruined our lives? Jimmy, and . . . and Lisa . . . Leave us alone, Montez. Please."

I stammered a response.

"Look here, why . . . uh, why don't you sit down? Here, at the table. You've got to believe me. I never hurt your son or daughter, and I'm not going to hurt you. But I guess you can't believe me."

She continued to cry into Greg's shoulder, and he simply stared over her head. I wasn't sure whether he was looking at me or a spot on the wall.

I plodded on.

"I didn't have anything to do with Jimmy's or Lisa's murders. I swear it. But even if you don't believe me, I still have to have some answers. I still need to ask you questions. And the sooner we get it over with, the sooner I leave, and the sooner you can call the cops. So, how long I'm here is basically up to you."

159

She cleared her throat. The crying was over, replaced with a focused hate.

"All right, you son of a bitch. What are your questions?"

I didn't waste time.

"What's your connection to Alton Enoch? How do you know him, and why?"

She shook her head in pity.

"I don't know Alton Enoch. I know the name. He's the man who was arrested with Jimmy. I've never seen him, don't know him. What else?"

"I saw you at his house. What are you covering up? What does he have over you? He's already killed Jimmy, and probably Lisa. What else can he do to you?"

Greg responded.

"She's telling the truth. Jimmy talked to me once about Enoch, when he was in jail, waiting for his hearing. He said that Enoch was going to walk away again. Something about how the juju king, or something like that, always walked away. I didn't understand what he meant. I still don't. But we don't know Enoch."

They both sounded sincere, and I knew they were lying. I wanted to badger them, to force them, somehow, to open up and level with me, but I couldn't do it. Enoch obviously was not someone they were ready to talk about, yet. However, now that Greg had found his voice, he wouldn't shut up.

"You killed Jimmy. It wasn't Enoch. Nothing you say can convince us otherwise. This is a pathetic ploy on your part, Montez. I hope the cops blow your fucking brains all over my front yard. I pray to God that happens."

"You may get an answer to your prayer, Esch. A few more things, first. How about Martinez and Strayhorn, the cops?"

Greg and Beatrice smiled, almost in unison, when the barking of their dogs interrupted my questions. The animals apparently had moved to the front of the house since they had been frustrated in their attempt to gnaw off my legs.

I listened to the dogs, straining for meaning in their growling, when a buzzer's shrill announcement made us all jump. I assumed a doorbell had been pushed by someone at the front gate.

"Time for me to leave. But listen to this. I am innocent. I haven't hurt you or your family. One day, I hope I can prove that. For now, all I can say is that I'm sorry for what has happened, to all of us."

I ushered them into a hall closet that had more space than my rented room. They sat on the floor, in response to my orders, and I left them curled together in a corner of coats and ski boots. I propped a chair against the doorknob and hoped that I had slowed them down enough to give me the time I needed to get out of the neighborhood.

The Dobermans were into full-blown watchdog frenzy. Whoever had stirred them up evidently did not care about waking the neighbors.

I slipped out the same door that I had flown through only a few minutes before. The dogs didn't know what to do. They jumped off a few yards in my direction as I made for the far recesses of the Eschs' backyard; then they switched their snarls to the new intruder. I made it to a back fence. I tore my pants, but I finally reached the top of the wooden beams that sat against what passed for an alley in this neighborhood, only a few yards from the bicycle path. I tossed Greg Esch's gun into a bush. I glanced back at the house. The front gate swung open and two people ran up the driveway. Mrs. Esch stood on the lawn, hollering hysterically, demanding that someone call the cops. So much for my chair idea. I didn't see Greg.

Just before I jumped into the darkness, I heard the new couple try to comfort Mrs. Esch.

Percival Jones said, "Hey, let us help. We're here to help. What happened?"

And Frances Jones said, "It's that damn Montez, Percival. Has to be. Get the cops. He can't be far away."

The bike path offered no cover, but plenty of room to run. I gave it all I had, for several miles. I pumped my legs and flailed my arms while I tried to keep my gun secure in my pants. I listened for sirens, and when I did meet another person on the path, I immediately prepared for the worst. A man who looked homeless ducked for cover when he saw me coming out of the night, and a young pair of lovers, arm in arm, scurried out of my way and plopped on a bench, where they watched me rush by.

I dropped in exhaustion somewhere in Arapahoe County. I tasted dirt. I rolled over on my back and stretched my cramping legs. My breath was heavy, sucking in pain. Sweat rolled off my forehead, into my eyes and mouth. Faint, cheerful points of light in the night sky mocked me.

And all I could think of was Perk and Frances. And nothing made any sense.

It took me several hours to walk back to the city. The spring night was cool and damp, and I had to run and walk briskly just to keep my blood from cooling down and clogging my heart. I used side roads, alleys, ditches—everything except the streets. Again, I was without wheels. I had deserted Evangelina's car, and it had to have been impounded by the cops who answered the Esch's cry for help. Tenorio had seized Lisa's car and there was no doubt that he was going through Evangelina's Honda with his usual precision.

I was on a streak.

The mix of Perk and Frances and Greg and Beatrice bothered me, of course. But it intrigued me more. Different possible scenarios popped up, played themselves out, and were replaced by others. Misty conclusions from the possibilities played with me as I weaved through fenced acreage waiting for the developers, or clung to the safety of trash

162

Dumpsters. I laughed out loud when I thought about my concerns for their well-being after I had left them hog-tied in Nevada. I took it as a good sign that I still had a sense of humor about my life.

I worried about Evangelina. She had always been intimidated by cops—a trait left over from growing up with her hell-raising stepsister, Jenny. As soon as the car was traced back to her, detectives and officers would be all over her, trying to squeeze what they could from my more-or-less-innocent former lover and secretary. The cops would pretend to know more than they really did, and she wouldn't know anything more than what my father or Chuey was able to funnel to her. Their help would be too late. It could come only after it was public knowledge that I was back in Denver, and her car had been found, and that would be hours after she would be questioned, maybe by Tenorio himself.

I hoped she had reported the car as stolen. She had to stick to that story, or take a rap for aiding a fugitive.

I had accomplished very little. All who tried to help me— family, ex-girlfriends, strangers on the highway who offered me a ride—had been burned, because of me.

Another streak intact.

I slithered into my apartment building about the same time as the sun sliced through the curtain. Each time I returned to my apartment, I expected to find someone— Tenorio, or Enoch, or the bloody spirit of one of the many victims of the killing spree. A creak in the floor surprised me when I would try to glide silently up to my front door with the hope that I could ambush whomever it was who surely waited for me. But that creak inevitably would erupt from under my left shoe, echo in the hall, and, I was certain, arouse everyone on the floor, including my anticipated guest. I tried to avoid the spot where I had concluded the creak rested, waiting for me, but I hit it anyway. So much for the element of ambush.

My room was locked, but I couldn't be sure that I had had no visitors. I took the chance, without giving it too much thought. I eased my way into my room without turning on the lights, and I thought that this could be another mistake, like failing to hide Evangelina's car away from the Esch house. The chill and exertion from my marathon walk had me stiff and shaky, and I almost wished that Tenorio would take me in just so I could get a few minutes of rest.

No one pounced on me, and I wasn't arrested. The room was as dreary as ever, and equally as empty.

My time had to be about up. Everyone knew I was back in Denver—Beatrice Esch, Wanda Higgins, Detective Tenorio. How long I had left on the streets could be measured in hours, if that. Higgins would broadcast my picture again, to remind the public what I looked like, and Tenorio would have extra uniforms and patrol cars running down every lead that might have something to do with me and my crime spree. He'd intrude, again, on the privacy of my father, and anyone else who might have contact with me—Chuey, Roberta, Ybarra—and try to force a break in the case. He'd do his job efficiently and zealously, unless I came up with something else first.

I had to force the hand of the killer.

17

The restaurant on East Colfax catered to hookers, dealers, misfits—and cops. On other nights—boozy, barhopping, greasy-breakfast nights—I had watched teams of officers saunter through the diner just to give the customers an extra thrill with their 3:00 A.M. coffee. Chuey knew about the joint, and although I ran the risk of bumping into an undercover cop or two, it was close to my room. I wouldn't have to be on the street too long, and I naïvely counted on my down-and-out appearance to cover up my "dodging the law" status. Gaunt men and pudgy women of all ages and races, looking a step or two short on the exhausting walk through life, wandered through the place, and I fit right in with that crowd. I thought that if I didn't make a ruckus, I should be relatively safe.

Once inside, I burrowed into a dark corner. I tried to melt into the shiny vinyl of an oily booth against the wall as I nursed coffee and a brittle Danish. Ten minutes after my arrival, my brother walked in and casually joined me in the booth.

He said, "I got your message."

I had relied on the code system I had set up with Jesús. We changed numbers and rings over the few days since I had returned to Denver, but it was a system that couldn't last. It was almost time for my final hand. I bet a good chunk of my emotional bankroll on a face-to-face with Chuey.

He ordered his own coffee, then turned his attention to me.

"You don't look good, Little Louie. Kind of wild, man. Almost bad enough to make me think that you *are* some kind of serial killer, someone who *could* use a knife on Glory Jane and Jimmy Esch."

"Thanks for the vote of confidence. I'm not doing well, bro. But I think I've got this thing under control. At least, I have a feeling about what I should do. How's Dad?"

"Better. Still shaky, but better. He's using a cane all the time now, and his good eye is fucking up. He doesn't have a lot of time, Louie. Whatever you're going to do, you better do it quick."

"It's almost over. The way I see it, the killer has to incriminate himself, do something even Ug Tenorio can figure out, something that adds up to two and two but doesn't equal Luis Montez. That's why I called you. I need your help, again."

He sat back in the booth and lit a cigarette.

"Sounds dangerous. What is it?"

I didn't stop to put in perspective Chuey's seemingly changed attitude about me. He was my brother—my malicious, jealous, asshole brother—but my brother, nevertheless, and I had called him under the assumption that if I couldn't get him to help, I might as well walk in the cop station and let Tenorio drag me away. It was up to him to disabuse me of any incorrect assumptions.

"It has to be Alton Enoch who's done the cutting. I looked up his record, his history, even talked with him for a few

166

minutes. These are the facts about him. He's an old hand with knives. He had a nice thing going with Martinez and Strayhorn, almost a vocation. He made an opportune phone call to one of the Keystone Kops, and that resulted in Jimmy's arrest, and my eventual appearance on Jimmy's behalf. But—and this is the part that's so slick, it's almost better than baby oil—all this time, Alton was working *with* Jimmy on a crazy game with bad cop Strayhorn."

"Whoa, man. Enoch had Esch busted, and then he helped Esch get to Strayhorn so that Esch would get off? Playing both sides like that is risky, risky. You really think Enoch is that smart?"

"Smarter than Esch, no doubt. I think Strayhorn got too squirrely for Enoch, so a convenient accident occurs. One of the trades he picked up during one of his several prison tours was auto mechanic. He might have known how to rig brakes or steering on that sap Strayhorn's car."

Chuey's face twisted into a grimace of appreciation. At least, that's how I took it. I rolled on.

"And who knows about Esch? When you think about it, Jimmy could have been done for a hundred different reasons that had nothing to do with his case. Junkies kill one another over dirty needles, Chuey. Or maybe Jimmy started to wise up. Maybe he suspected that Enoch had tipped off the cops. He calls Enoch on it, talks bad and acts stupid, and Enoch takes care of him."

"A matter of rep, huh, or standing in the community, so to speak?"

"It's easy for me to put it together that way."

"But you told me once about the money angle. The Eschs are loaded. Doesn't that have anything to do with this? And Glory Jane? What about her?"

"Glory Jane knew the whole picture; I'm convinced of that. She was about to tell me about the arrest, and the relationship between Enoch and the cops. Enoch knew she was a risk, and he unfortunately found her the same night I did."

"Unfortunately for both of you."

I nodded and finished off my coffee.

"The money, Louie. It's got to have some bearing on this."

"Well, what I found out from Padgett and the little bit Ybarra dug up is that Lisa was the only one, other than Jimmy, who could benefit from the trust apparatus. As the sister, she would get most of what Jimmy had coming to him, if he violated the terms of the trust, or croaked. It was set up so that if Jimmy or Lisa fucked up, then the other one got the fuckup's share. But killing Jimmy wasn't necessary for that. He was a loser, and it was obvious to everyone except his mother that eventually he would have ended up with nothing, all on his own. I can't believe Lisa was money-hungry enough to go after her brother, especially when it was apparent she didn't have to."

Chuey chimed in. "And she's another victim in this whole mess, *pobrecita*. I agree. The killing of Jimmy Esch only makes sense like they almost always do—just one punk killing another one. But what happened to Lisa?"

"She got too close to the truth about her brother's killing. I left her that morning, and she didn't know a damn thing about Jimmy or Strayhorn. Take my word for it, she didn't. No one knew Jimmy had been killed, except the killer, of course, until I stumbled across his body later that afternoon. By then, Lisa was either kidnapped or dead, too. She found out something and tried to deal with it on her own—with Enoch. Eventually, her body turns up in the mountains."

"You haven't been charged with that, have you?"

"Ybarra thinks that the DA and the cops know they can wait. They don't have any physical evidence to link me to her death, but they do have my trip out west and a few of my other guilty-looking acts. Galena and Tenorio have time. After they get their hands back around my neck, they can squeeze a couple of confessions out of me, including one for Lisa. That's Ricardo's assessment, and it sounds right to me."

"I don't know, Louie. You're laying everything on Alton Enoch. Are you sure?"

I smiled for the first time in days.

"No way! I'm not sure of anything. There are questions I still have, answers I don't have. I don't know why Beatrice Esch visited Enoch at midnight. I'm not sure why Martinez left town like his butt was on fire. And there's this odd pair of con artists I met on the road—they have something to do with this, but I sure as hell don't know what. Yeah, there's plenty I can't scope out. That's why I've got to have something happen. That's why I called you."

"So, what is it, Little Louie? What's the big plan, man?"

I went through the details. Chuey thought it was iffy at best. I asked him to be my backup, which meant taking a chance on me and my crazy idea. That chance could cost him his life. He finally agreed when I made it clear that I was going ahead with it and that he could help or not. It was his choice, but I didn't really have any.

He stood to leave, assuring me that he had it right. He reached for my hand and shook it. I felt uncomfortable when I grasped his hand, and a sense of regret washed over me. Irrationally, I missed Chuey.

I left the booth's security and walked into the glitzy, frantic night of East Colfax. Neon slashes and police spotlights provided ephemeral illumination for a scene straight out of a Bukowski poem. Unspecific shouts, blasting car boombox music that shook storefront windows, screams, sirens, thuds, and squealing brakes smothered conversations. City noise throbbed a kaleidoscopic beat down dead-end alleys

169

and over double-parked travelers lost in their own nightmare gridlock. Traffic heading nowhere clogged the street, and pedestrians swarmed in defensive groups.

I was the only man who walked alone. A trio of bearded, sleazy boys in tough leather and mean body ornaments swaggered across the sidewalk and bumped into a woman I assumed earned her rent as a prostitute. She promptly began a tirade of vulgarity and blasphemous oaths. The three laughed, grabbed her, slapped their hands up and down her cheaply perfumed body, then pushed her into the street. She planted her long knifelike fingernails on her miniskirted hips and kept at her name-calling until the rude guys crossed the intersection. I thought she was Native American or Asian, but she could have been a Chicana.

When at last I lay on the bed, smoking a cigarette and listening to the fucking going on next door, I easily understood that everything I had told Chuey could have been wrong, and that if he wasn't careful, he, too, would die, and it would be my fault—as they all were.

I waited two days for something to happen. Chuey had to talk with Ybarra; then the media types had to package Ybarra's announcement properly. The two days passed without me leaving the room except for a late-night run for beer and a sandwich. On the third day, Friday, I was gone with the sunrise. I found a newspaper machine and quickly confirmed that my plan was in motion.

Halfway down the front page, Ricardo Ybarra looked intently into the reader's face. The headline under his photo proclaimed: FUGITIVE LAWYER TO TURN SELF IN. A second line read, in smaller type: *Montez Promises Revelations—Will Implicate Others.*

I waited until I returned to the apartment to read the entire story. It was good. Ybarra had arranged for me to show up at Galena's office on Saturday afternoon. The article didn't mention him, but I assumed Tenorio was also expected. My lawyer had laid it on pretty good for the press. Chuey must have had quite an effect on Ricardo.

Ybarra was quoted extensively. He explained: "I have always known that my client Luis Montez has been innocent of the terrible crimes he has been accused of. Unfortunately, innocent men are often charged and, yes, even convicted. Although I did not know of his plans, and I did not approve of them after I knew what he had been doing, Luis took it upon himself to bring about justice in his case." Good CYA, Ricardo. "I am happy to announce that he now has irrefutable proof of his innocence. He intends to turn over his evidence to the district attorney and cooperate completely in the prosecution of those who are responsible for the brutal deaths of James Esch, Lisa Esch, and Glory Jane Jacquez. Those of us who are friends and colleagues of Mr. Montez can rejoice that this sad, horrible miscarriage of the legal system is about over."

The article also quoted DA Galena. He offered that as far as he was concerned, "Luis Montez is a murderer and a disgrace to the legal profession. This grandstand play is a cheap trick to garner sympathy and an attempt to distract my office and the police. But it won't work. We have been prepared to try Montez for his crimes and we intend to do just that. As far as turning himself in, that's the best advice his lawyer gave him, but it won't make us ease up securing a conviction against him for his heinous crimes. As long as he is a fugitive, Montez is a very real threat and danger to the public, and the police have orders to treat him as such."

I took his closing comment to mean that it was still open season on Luis Montez until I planted my butt in Galena's office. I hoped Tenorio didn't plan to use the opportunity to finish me off on the steps of the DA's building.

Then, I waited again. I had to deal with Friday night, then Saturday morning, and, I had to assume, somewhere I would face Enoch and one more confrontation. It would have to be near Galena's office. I wanted to be as obvious as possible.

I stayed in my room, thinking that I was near the end of the Esch case, finally. I started to relax. I told myself that there was no more reason to be neurotic about my paranoia. There *had* to be a killer after me now, and that was reassuring. In a matter of hours, I would be done with this—one way or the other.

18

◆

It must have been around four in the morning when the creak in the hallway woke me. Up until that second when I twitched in my saggy bed, no one had confirmed my theory about the worn-out floor's ability to serve as a security alarm. Sometimes, I hate it when I'm right.

Without thinking about the consequences, I grabbed Frances's .38 from the nightstand, then gently slid to the floor and crawled under the bed. Dust balls, clumps of petrified mud, and discarded tissue seemed to rush at me and cling to my face and hair. I moved the gun to my right hand and waited for my visitor.

I heard movement at the door handle, but it was brief and to the point. The door opened for just an instant, letting in a sliver of gray light that scarred the room's complete darkness. The heavy curtain stretched across the window, blocking out everything from Colfax except an occasional siren or hysterical wail. In the silence, I could not hear the intruder; he was in the room, probably staring at my empty bed. A form in the shape of a shoe scraped along the floor, directly in front of my face. My eyes adjusted and focused on the form.

It was tight under the bed, and I knew I could not make a quick move. I had to time my steps. I had to wait for the person to turn his back; then I would leap and hope and pray that I could hang on to Alton Enoch, and dodge his thirsty knife blade until someone called the cops.

He moved closer to the bed. The shoes turned a half twist to the north—checking out the room, trying to imagine where I could be. It was as plain as the dead cockroach that rested near my chin. There was only one possible place—under the bed.

How had Enoch found my room? I had expected him to make his move when I finally showed my face in public. Chuey had cautioned that I would be a sitting duck for a shooting outside of Galena's building, and I agreed, but I didn't have anything better to offer. But even a sitting duck sounded better than a prostrate worm stuffed under a two-bit bed.

There was something wrong with the shoes. They were ordinary athletic shoes, but they bothered me as I tried to keep them in my range of vision. When they disappeared, I told myself to get a grip. Do something, Montez. I slid backward, inching my way from under the bed. It was taking too long, and the longer it took for me to extricate myself from my hiding place, the more I felt Enoch's blade separating my neck from my shoulders.

I lost any sense of patience. I muttered, "Fuck it!" I gave up the inching and hurtled myself into the black room.

I immediately rolled into my visitor. I heard a scream from somewhere. The gun interfered with what I had to do, but I gripped it tightly anyway. I wrestled with the stranger, and, with my left hand, I grabbed a thin, soft neck and started to twist.

"Montez . . ."

I heard my name from the choked neck, and I knew then what had bothered me about the shoes. They were too small to fit on Alton Enoch's feet. As I squeezed, I thought I remembered the softness of that neck.

I jerked the head around and confronted the eyes of Beatrice Esch. I dropped her and she fell to the floor. What the hell was Mrs. Esch doing? I bent down to ask her, and then I knew why Mrs. Esch had denied visiting Alton Enoch at midnight. Mrs. Esch was much older than the woman who lay at my feet, and her hair was not as brilliant, and her face was not as pretty.

I stared at the unconscious figure of Lisa Esch. My hands shook and my lips formed incoherent syllables. The gun clattered to the floor. I didn't know what to do. I couldn't see if she was breathing.

The sound outside the room almost grabbed my attention, but it was so small a creak that it couldn't compete with Lisa Esch's sprawled body. But I did pay attention to the slamming door. The problem was, by the time I realized it was the door to my apartment, my head had been smashed by what the newspapers label a blunt instrument, Lisa's body had dreamily floated up to me, and I had curled up next to her. I slipped into unconsciousness as her hands caressed my face. I missed the part where my wrists were tied behind my back and my mouth was covered with duct tape and I was manhandled out of my apartment and thrown into the trunk of a car. Somewhere in all of that, I concluded that my plan hadn't quite worked out.

19

---◆---

The thing about duct tape is that it draws tighter the longer it's affixed to skin. My lips were squeezed shut, and my jawbone strained against the unnatural lock on my mouth. I persuaded myself that things could be worse—at least my eyes were unobstructed. It wasn't much as I rolled on my side in the total darkness.

I was in a small room, maybe a closet. My feet and hands were bound, but by turning on my stomach, I measured the space with my shoulders and legs and bumped into objects whose identity I guessed at—a bucket, a broom, a pile of newspapers.

From outside the darkness, music floated and drifted around me—sweet, exuberant music. Violins reacted to a conductor's vision with impressive—exquisite—performances. Without wanting to, I recognized an allegro by Vivaldi—one of the few classical composers I could name. I didn't stay with the music for long.

Crushing pain encircled my head. I couldn't see it, but dried blood outlined a gash on the back of my skull. I didn't know how much time had passed while I had been out. I remembered Lisa. She wasn't in the closet.

Nausea overcame me. On the floor, with my body cramped and bound, my mind fixed on unreal visions and expectations. I wasn't dizzy, but I had a hell of an orientation problem, and I couldn't escape the sensation of falling. The darkness covered me like a coat of tar and the brink of hysteria crept into my space. I fought against the queasiness. The duct tape would guarantee that I would drown in my vomit. A shrieking violin stabbed at my skull, and what had been a sentimental melody transformed itself into a piercing, tortuous din. The struggle for control made me sweat. I kicked my feet into empty, futile space. The pain escalated. Panic won. The space was too dark, too small, and I couldn't move, couldn't breathe. I passed out.

I woke when my lips were ripped off. I twitched in distress, blinded by sudden light. My eyes watched, without really seeing, a dainty red-haired peacock finger pieces of my mouth. Nerve endings cautiously responded and the scene came into focus.

A blue Mardi Gras mask shielded her eyes with feathers, rhinestones, and gaudy beads. The mask should have enhanced her ethereal beauty, but for me it only accented the danger she represented. Her uncovered mouth and lips made a swirl in the pea soup that used to be my brain.

If what she did with that dress can be called wearing, then she wore a black evening gown. Her shoulders and the upper half of her bosom were naked, and the dress was shorter than most of the ties I carelessly draped around my professional neck. The red hair was less full than I remembered, and the face more weary. But Lisa was as intriguing as the night I had camped out in her bedroom, so many lifetimes ago.

177

She had removed the tape from my face with more energy than necessary, but I could breathe easier. She held my face in her hands and offered me a glass of water.

"You're awake. Finally. The drugs must be wearing off."

"What . . . what the hell . . ."

"We don't have much time. You've been drugged for hours. It's Saturday night. I know nothing makes sense, but you have to trust me. Try to listen, Louie. We need to get out of here, before—"

Someone walked in the room. Lisa let my head drop. She moved away from me.

"Ah, Montez, you're back with us. Just in time for the ball."

He daintily held a gleaming CD. He slipped it into his streamlined machine on the wall as he talked. Vivaldi rolled over us and my nausea threatened to return.

He wore a tuxedo and a mask similar to Lisa's, except his colors were red and black. A red-and-black cummerbund fit in with his red-and-black bow tie and his red-and-black mask. He reached into his jacket and flourished a thin golden stiletto. He flicked his wrist ever so slightly, and the blade slipped into position and locked. He made sure I saw his knife.

"We'll be late, but that's all right. You know how these things are, don't you? Maybe you don't, actually. The Barristers Benefit Ball? It's such a good cause. Raising thousands of dollars for pro bono lawyers for the poor and incapacitated. One of my favorite events of the year. I thought it would be very appropriate for your final appearance. Though I can't say I always appreciate the choice of themes. This year, it's Magical Masquerade, but then, you can probably figure that out from the way we're decked out."

The tuxedo somebody had pushed me into was a couple of sizes too big, but it was clean. With more effort than it should have taken, I touched my face. No mask.

"Plenty of your old friends will be at the ball. You have some amends to make, Louie. You let down so many important people today when you didn't show for your well-publicized meeting with DA Galena. And you know how that man is."

I croaked out a few words.

"Ball? Friends?"

He ignored my croaking.

"Contrary to the popular perception, lawyers are a generous, charitable lot. Ybarra, Galena. Judge Bernstein. They'll be there. And rich do-gooders from across the city, including your close friends, Mr. and Mrs. Esch. Almost a reunion, of sorts, don't you think, Montez?"

Lisa flinched at the mention of her parents. She sat on the couch, next to me. I apparently had been flat on my back, unconscious. I was groggy and thirsty as hell. I mouthed words, but my lips wouldn't quite function. Talking was no longer automatic. Finally, my labor paid off with a couple of sentences.

"Can you . . . turn down . . . music? Bitch of . . . headache."

He smiled. He played with his knife too carelessly, I thought. He sliced the air with a vicious couple of jabs.

"So droll, Montez, even in the face of absolute disaster. I've always liked that about you. Honestly, I thought your skewed outlook would help you when you lost the Esch case, but then, as we all know now, somehow, you didn't lose. Your bad luck, and, as it turned out, that of a few others. Your patchwork lawyering made this operation much more difficult than it should have been. Still, I think everything will turn out, don't you, my dear?"

Lisa stared at me. She didn't respond to him.

Again, I tried talking. It was slightly easier.

"What is this? What . . . fuck . . . you doing . . . Padgett?"

I tried to stand, but I couldn't make it. My legs wobbled

and quaked when I tried to use them. I fell to one knee.

"Louie, please, don't try. You're awake enough to do what I want you to do, and nothing else. You can't do anything except what we help you to do. If you insist on trying, you will only make yourself sick, and we don't have time to clean you up. And, you might get hurt."

The knife did another job to the air.

"If we leave now, we should make it just as the Eschs are arriving. Then you'll be on your own. Then you can try whatever you want."

He finished with laughter that grew with intensity each time he took a breath. He appeared to lose control. He bent over, choking off his guffaws while his torso gyrated and twisted. After a few minutes, he quit, returning his attention to Lisa and me. A tear ran from under his mask.

"We should be going. Lisa, help him to the car."

He was right about at least one thing. I couldn't do much without someone's help. With great difficulty, I stood and leaned on Lisa's arm. Padgett walked behind us, inches away from my back. I remembered that when I was drunk, I would overcome obstacles that I could never handle while sober, although the details were always fuzzy after those excursions. The jaunt from Padgett's office to his parking garage was in the same category as my drunken wobbling, except for the fact that I hadn't been drinking, and I didn't have to wait for the morning after to forget the details.

Lisa steered me out of Padgett's office, down the elevator, and through the parking garage, until we came to his car. I thought I had been walking for hours.

The car was a roomy four-door Chrysler. I crawled into the backseat, out of breath and weak. Lisa drove while Padgett sat next to me, the knife occasionally scratching my neck.

I forced my mind to concentrate. I formed words and pushed them through frozen lips.

"You sent Esch . . . to me . . . to lose. You . . . rotten . . ."

The knife pressed against the front of my throat.

"Easy, Louie. I can always say that you attacked me, just as you attacked Jimmy boy, and Glory Jane, and Martinez, and even the Eschs. I'd rather you go out in a barrage of bullets from Tenorio and his buddies, but if you force me, I won't hesitate to use my rather sharp friend on you here and now."

He moved his knife across my Adam's apple. The sting helped clear away a few of the cobwebs.

"All this for . . . Jimmy's share . . . Esch estate?"

Lisa had taken off the mask to drive the car. She caught my eye in the rearview mirror.

"It's more than that, Louie. He wants it all. He wants all the goddamn money, property, businesses. Jimmy was only the beginning."

My body sagged even more. Padgett relaxed.

"Oh, I'll get what I want. And up until the deal got a little rough, Ms. Lisa Esch was in it with me, all the way. She wanted her hands on the folks' nest egg almost as badly as I did. She did what she had to. Helped set up her brother. Made sure he had the dope when he was supposed to. And if he had been convicted, Lisa and I would have been well on our way. But, well-laid plans and all that."

Lisa shouted at him. "Stop it! It wasn't like that! . . ." Her voice trailed off. "Please, stop."

"Now, now, Lisa. Let's not be revisionist about this. You see, Louie, Lisa dear offered the only way I could ever share in her wealth. Poor thing fell in love with the wrong guy— me. Even married me one wild night. She denies it, but I've got the paperwork, witnesses. All legal and tidy. When she finally came out of her daze, it was too late, and she was in too deep. I think she doesn't want to see anybody else die. But, realistically, what is she going to do about it?"

The knots in my guts tightened up. I *had* roused the

killer. He planned to have me wasted out in the open, at the Barristers Ball, where I would be an easy target for cops and hotel security. He would force the cops to shoot me with a couple of errant bullets that looked as though they were coming from me, as I stumbled up to the Eschs. Maybe they would be hit in the volley of bullets. Maybe he could take care of two problems at once. He might even do the deed himself, play the hero. Lisa eventually would have to be removed. He had to have something in mind for her, too, later, when they were alone.

"Crazy. No way . . . will work."

"Calm down, Louie. You'll bust your bow tie. Jimmy was like that, too. What an excitable guy! Couldn't understand what Lisa and I were up to. He had to be silenced. Not that I planned that. I simply wanted to get to the bottom of the Strayhorn testimony, but he played dumb, too dumb for his own good. He got carried away and I had to defend myself, that's all."

Lisa's outburst surprised both Padgett and me. "You liar! After Louie won the case, the only thing you could think of was getting rid of Jimmy. You killed him, and it wasn't the way you said. It wasn't!"

"Control, Lisa. Easy. You see things your way; I've got my version. I will admit that Jimmy's demise made it easier, though. His share went automatically to Lisa, and me, naturally. Jimmy's dying was about the only way left for us to get to his trust, after you screwed up my first idea, Louie. But, no hard feelings. And, I think it was better, the way it turned out. For example, the knife work . . . well, Mr. Enoch had outplayed his usefulness, and it seemed appropriate to drag him into this affair. A knife has been his logo, his trademark. I figured he would take the fall, and, truthfully, who would care? And then, lo and behold! You go and show up. How resourceful of you to blunder into Jimmy's apartment and offer yourself as a sacrificial lamb. Lisa and I couldn't have been more pleased."

My legs had regained some of their usefulness, and I knew I could talk if I had to. Sporadically, my brain let off flashes of cognition. For example, although I didn't ask Padgett for confirmation, I understood that Lisa had arranged our passionate get-together to keep me out of the way, to prevent any interference just in case Jimmy wised up and wanted to talk with his lawyer when Padgett met with him. She must have thought Padgett was only going to talk with him, try to get the truth out of him about Strayhorn. I didn't want to accept that she had planned to have her brother murdered.

Padgett was in a contemplative mood.

"We shouldn't be too harsh on Lisa. She has a terrible habit of poking her body with needles full of harsh, mind-altering drugs. She's so obviously a victim. We can't really blame her, can we, Louie?"

My grunt was noncommittal. Lisa's eyes were watery, but she didn't give me any more meaningful looks. She was too busy guiding Padgett's car through downtown traffic. We were near the hotel where the ball was scheduled. It was only a few blocks from Padgett's office. Any other night, we would have walked.

He directed Lisa to pull the car over to the curb, in a loading zone whose meter was covered with a bag that read FOR CONSTRUCTION TRUCKS ONLY. We watched traffic pull up to the front of the hotel, under an overhang where doormen and valets greeted the arriving guests. TV lights played over the revelers. At one of the hotel's revolving doors, Wanda Higgins interviewed the president of the bar association.

Padgett had Lisa join me in the backseat, where he quietly, expertly tied her hands behind her back.

Padgett smirked as he forced her to squeeze onto the floor.

"Too bad. All dressed up, and can't go to the ball. Maybe next year, my dear." His laugh was beginning to get on my nerves.

Ten minutes passed. A tender sliver of consciousness replaced the dull screen of the drug Padgett had given me. I tried to think of something to do.

Abruptly, he opened the door and yanked me to the side of the car.

"They're here. Let's go, Montez. Now!"

The knife jabbed my arm. He pulled me in the direction of the hotel. We were only a few yards away from the limousine that Padgett had recognized as the Eschs'. I mumbled, looked around, but he continued to force me toward the hotel. Cars lined up in anticipation of space under the overhang. The limo stopped near a red-coated man, who opened the door and waited for the passengers to exit. Mrs. Esch stepped out, resplendent in diamonds. Greg followed. Padgett pulled a gun from his coat pocket. I thought he was aiming at Mrs. Esch. I tried to jerk away, but he held the knife at my side. He pointed the gun at the sky. He was ready to pull the trigger, then leap away and leave me to the cops.

"So long, Louie."

I shouted, "Watch out! Gun! Gun!" Some in the crowd turned, but most ignored me.

Padgett fired his gun.

Mrs. Esch cringed, then collapsed to the ground. She saw me. She screamed and pointed at me. I stood in the street, alone. I was still groggy from my hours in the closet and the influence of Padgett's ministrations. The TV lights turned on me. I watched the people run and scream and fall. I had a wide-angle view of the spectacle.

In one corner of the extrawide picture, Wanda Higgins

furiously described the action for her camera.

Lisa's shout was loud and clear.

"Mother! Run! Run!"

Ignacio Tenorio's voice was almost drowned out by Lisa's frantic cries.

"Padgett! Drop the gun!"

Mrs. Esch screamed again. A shot blasted through the downtown canyons of steel and chrome and cardboard sleeping bags. I couldn't tell if the bullet had been meant for me. I drilled my body into the asphalt. I turned my face and saw Padgett aim his gun at Lisa, who continued to run to her mother.

"Mother! Watch out! Mother!"

The words didn't carry, but I read them off Padgett's lips.

"Good night, baby. Good night."

A puff of fire belched from his hand. His arm jerked backward. I didn't hear the shot. Lisa twirled in the air, landed on her feet, then stumbled. She clutched her chest, but she didn't stop. Thin rope dangled from her wrist. Padgett stared at her, marveling at the woman he had dragged into his personal hell. She fell into him and held on. He raised his gun to shoot her again.

I looked back where I thought I had heard Tenorio. He was in the middle of a wild mob who had rushed from the hotel. Tuxedos, furs, masks, and sequins bounced around him and his gun. He couldn't get free.

I forced myself to my feet. I told my legs to run to the wrestling Lisa and Padgett. I thought I was running. I couldn't reach them. He looked up from Lisa and saw me lurching in their direction. Delicately, purposefully, he aimed the gun at me. He smiled.

My knee exploded. My useless leg flew out from under me and collapsed. I shuddered, fell on my back. Blood oozed from the tuxedo pants.

I strained against the pain to keep my eyes on Lisa.

185

Blood covered her bare shoulders and had soaked the front of her dress. She lunged at him. The golden handle of the stiletto quivered in his stomach. Lisa Esch and David Padgett fell in a heap on the sidewalk.

Ybarra appeared in the space between two skyscrapers. He reached out to me and raised my head.

"Easy, Louie. You're going into shock. Easy. Hang on, man."

I hung on.

20

Detective Tenorio sat in a corner of my hospital room, thumbing a pile of magazines and newspapers. Lawyer Ybarra stood next to my bed, shaking his head. The big, ugly Chicano cop and the brainy, classy Chicano attorney had arranged a cooperative visit so they could clear up a few points. Ybarra was still my lawyer. There were several complications with my criminal cases that required his continuing services, including ironing out a few wrinkles with a bail bondsman who had asserted a claim to the deeds of my father's home and mine. But there was at least the expectation that one day it would be over.

Janice Kendall was dealing with what was left of my professional standing. It would take months, maybe years, before I could return as a member in good standing of the bar.

Tenorio was with me, too, but not necessarily for my own good.

The guy kept busy, I had to say that. The news article in his hand trumpeted Ug's arrest of Alton Enoch's girlfriend, Rochelle, for the murder of Glory Jane Jacquez. Alton had arranged a deal for himself that included packaging his roommate for her impetuous resolution of their love triangle. Still, he was on his way for his own cool stretch in Cañon City. Strayhorn wasn't around to protect him, and his multifaceted business affairs had finally caught up with him. The police department honchos breathed easier when the steel doors clanged shut behind the Juju Man.

The cop quit reviewing his personal publicity and joined Ricardo at my bedside.

I asked him something that I had thought about almost continuously as I recuperated from Padgett's marksmanship.

"When did you know that wasn't Lisa's body up in the mountains?"

"Almost immediately. Lab boys cleared that up. We didn't let that out. Too much going on. A judgment call, a way to play with the killer's head. And she called me."

His infuriating way of talking hadn't improved.

"You fucking knew?" I could only shake my head.

"Hell yes. We couldn't figure you out. You ran like a scared *conejo*. San Diego Department kept an eye on you for us, for a time."

The low-rider—a cop.

I turned my attention to Ybarra.

"Did you know about that, Ricardo?"

"No, Louie, I didn't. The detective and his pals kept me in the dark about her and about watching you. But everyone assumed you were in California. The cops out there tailed Evangelina and then waited for you to pick up her car. But they lost you on the freeway, when you tried to run Martinez off the road."

"And Lisa?"

"She apparently contacted this guy right after you flew the coop. From what I can piece together, she went through a real change of heart. Enoch told us that she visited him one night, all strung out, high and crazy, asking questions about Jimmy and Padgett and you. He calmed her down then got rid of her. She was probably trying to piece everything together, but her whacked-out head wouldn't let her. She decided she couldn't let you take the rap. She'd been hiding out from Padgett after he iced Jimmy—sometimes with her parents, sometimes on her own. She refused to turn herself in. But she told Tenorio that you didn't have anything to do with any murders. And I take it that Ignacio here at least informed the parents that the body in the mountains wasn't their daughter's."

Tenorio absentmindedly nodded—just another day at the office.

"And yet, you kept after me, kept the heat on? What the fuck for, Ug?"

"Not Ug. Ignacio. And how was I supposed to know Miss Esch was true? You were acting guilty across country. You *could* have been the guy."

"Right. Jesus Christ, I—"

Ricardo stopped me.

"Don't, Luis. It's over. Time to move on."

I didn't answer. Ricardo told Tenorio that they should leave and let me rest. The door shut behind them, and still I didn't say anything.

Yeah, move on. But Lisa couldn't move on.

I tried to sleep. I quit when I knew it was no good. I had to sort it out, again.

Lisa had been suckered into a wild scheme to get at Jimmy's money, by Padgett, her lover and drug connection. He wanted all that wealth that he knew intimately but that he could never have, no matter how much he skimmed in inflated fees, costs, and expenses. He sold Lisa on the frame of Jimmy, and it would have worked, except for Thomas Strayhorn and his strange testimony.

I had stumbled on that a hundred times since she had

died, and, finally, it came to me. She had bribed Strayhorn; she had relented in her greed and bought a way out for her brother. But her act of misguided mercy had enraged Padgett, and eventually resulted in Jimmy's death.

And Padgett could have arranged for Strayhorn's flight through a thousand feet of frozen mountain air, or it could have been an accident. Or—and this was what Martinez had whimpered when he finally faced up to it, with a bit of help from Frances's gun—Officer Strayhorn just got tired—sick and tired of his sorry career as a law-enforcement officer on the take. Depending on one's perspective, Monarch Pass can be exactly the right place to get tired.

After the decision in the Esch case, Padgett didn't have any more control. Lisa vanished, afraid for her own life. She didn't have the guts to turn herself in, but she did make a few telephone calls to Tenorio. Yet, she couldn't stay away from Padgett. Drugs brought her back to him, and they both found me.

Padgett's offer to help on my case had been accepted and he was allowed access to Ricardo's files. When I had set my plan in motion, Chuey had given Ricardo the address to my apartment, just in case something happened to the meeting with Galena. David Padgett found that address in Ricardo's office. He didn't know what to do except respond to my bait. But he knew enough not to wait for my timing. He concocted the bizarre finale at the Barristers Ball. He was insane, too far gone to know that his plan could never work, even if I were finished off.

The hospital room was filled with books and games from Jesús. They were mostly leftovers from his own recent stay at Denver General. From the Arizona desert, Jesús Montez, Jr., had sent a pint of tequila disguised as a box of chocolate-covered cherries.

Somewhere amid the boxes and papers was a card from a former employee.

"Guess you're going to make it. I can put away my candle now. Take care. Evie. P.S. You owe me a car."

I moved timidly through the hospital's side door, wary and sore, and on crutches. I wasn't sure if I should expect Wanda Higgins or Ug Tenorio. A cab waited, but Perk and Frances Jones stopped me before I could climb in.

"Hey, Montez. Remember us?"

Perk grinned, while Frances stood off to his side. He wore a clean-cut pair of slacks and a button-down sport shirt. Frances also had reached for the mainstream look. She was a bit off the mark. Her yellow stretch pants didn't stretch quite enough, and her sleek white tank top was . . . perfect. She had changed the color of her hair. A bouncy mix of copper glints and blond streaks finished off what for her had to be a matronly approach to style.

I looked them over quickly for guns or knives.

"What do you want?"

"Hey, buddy. Is that any way to greet old friends?"

"Friends? I don't think so."

"If anybody should have hard feelin's, it should be us. The last time we saw you wasn't exactly on the best of terms."

Frances moved in front of Perk.

She said, "You bastard. We could have died out there in the desert. We were lucky, and so were you. For your own good, it turned out all right."

"All right! Amazing, fucking amazing! You come around to kiss and make up? And what the hell were you doing at the Esch house? At least I think it was you."

Some of the finer points of the past several weeks had lost their glow. Already, the memories had dulled.

Perk offered an attempt at an explanation. "Well, the truth of the matter is . . . well, it's like this, you see . . ."

Frances took over.

191

"We don't want to talk about the Esch family. That was a big miscalculation on our part, a real misunderstanding. And, well, now there are charges for some kind of fraud or extortion, something that we don't entirely understand. It's just a misunderstanding, won't take much to put a stop to it, but I guess the bottom line, Montez, the bottom line is, we need a lawyer, and we thought that . . . well, maybe, seeing as how you do kind of owe us . . ."

"*¡Qué chingada! ¡Madre de Dios!* This is really too much. You want me to act as your lawyer? What next? What could possibly be next?"

I awkwardly took advantage of the cabbie's open door, then directed him to my father's house. Before we drove away, I briefly and patiently explained to Perk and Frances that my ability to practice law was on a temporary hold, which I personally expected to have cleared up soon. But, meanwhile, if they needed a real good criminal defense attorney, I happened to know one who would do everything he could for them. I gave them Ricardo's card. By the time we separated, we were sentimental about old times, and we promised to look each other up, in Vegas, one of these days.

Jesús ambled up the ramp on our way to our seats in section 512 of Mile High Stadium. His cane clattered against the concrete, almost as loudly as my own cane. The two of us rested. We leaned against a cold wall. It was late September, the final home game for the Rockies, and although it was a warm, pleasant day, fall was close, and that meant winter was not so far away. Our favorite player, Armando Reynoso, was scheduled to pitch. It was the first game either one of us had been able to attend.

Jesús said, "Damn, Louie. If we keep climbing, I'm going to need my oxygen. Are we at a baseball game, or is this Pikes Peak? Damn, this is high."

"Just don't start talking about kites and poker games."

192

The Rockies were thirty-four games out of first place, but the stadium was clogged with another record crowd. The roar and buzz of the fans excited me, churned my blood and made me regret even more the ache and misery of my shattered leg. My father and I were a duet of grumbling, hobbled Chicanos who were still walking in the aisle when "The Star-Spangled Banner" finished.

We shoved our way to our seats, a couple of miles from home plate. The players took the field, and we could almost make out the numbers on their uniforms. I ordered a beer and the old man munched on a hot dog. We carefully rested our canes at our feet. The sun forced me out of my denim jacket. I leaned back in the seat and listened for the crack of the bat. I stretched my injured leg and rubbed the muscles with the hope that whatever was left of summer would stimulate the blood and speed up the healing process. My father tried to pay attention to the game, but he drifted in and out of sleep.

I was at the summit of a mountain of seventy thousand people. Everywhere there was shouting, cheering, laughter. A brother and sister compared Galarraga, Bichette, and Hayes. The scoreboard flashed runs, hits, and errors from around the country, and a fervent fan in the row in front of us listened to the game on a portable radio while he memorialized the particulars with a pencil and scorecard. Below us, next to the field and in the more expensive seats, in the boxes and reserved sections, lawyers and judges downed large cups of beer as they whistled and clapped for the team. I could almost hear them speculate on who would return next year, make childish side bets for each inning, and call no one in particular on their cellular phones. A pair of unused binoculars hung around my neck. I didn't see anybody I knew near our seats, and I didn't scan for a familiar face.

I had made it to a baseball game. I had survived. I didn't

track the specifics of the action on the field, but the game was the greatest game I would ever watch. Rivulets of sweat flowed from under my baseball cap and spread across the back of my shirt. Thin streams of tears traced their way down my face. I let myself go with the crowd. I turned invisible. The Chicano lawyer without a license, the once-infamous fugitive and suspected killer, the man who seemed out of place anywhere in the country—I connected to the proud and constant American game of baseball. I soared with the cheers and clamor, covered myself with the game's simplicity and truth, succumbed to the warmth of the day, and not once did I think about Jimmy Esch, or Glory Jane Jacquez, or Lisa.

Not once.

RAP   MYSTERY

JUN 2 1 1996